BAD BLOOD

BAD BLOOD

BY CARLY ANNE WEST
ART BY TIM HEITZ AND ARTFUL DOODLERS

Scholastic Inc.

ISBN 978-1-338-59428-7

10 9 8 7 6 5 4 3 2 1   20 21 22 23 24
Printed in the U.S.A   23
First printing 2020

Book design by Cheung Tai

PROLOGUE

He isn't afraid until the sky turns purple.

"Please," he says. "I didn't see anything."

But in the forest, it's the trees that seem to decide what gets seen and heard. Tonight, his words are buried.

"I promise I won't tell."

He hesitates only for a moment. Then he hears the first footstep.

He's fast, but they're faster. Each time his boots hit the ground, leaves crunch behind him, closing the distance between them.

A bramble loops around his ankle, and he goes down hard, smacking his chin, his teeth squeezing the sides of his tongue. Gasping, he crawls to his feet again, launching forward, flailing through low branches and reaching vines. He bursts out of the thicket and into the clearing. Still, the moonlight can't break through. It's like the sky has swallowed it.

They're coming.

He whips around, frantically searching for a place to hide, and dives behind a nearby bulldozer, its massive shovel still entrenched in the soft ground. Crawling underneath the scoop, he tugs his knees to his chest, struggling to hold his breath before he's had a chance to catch it.

Now he can see a sliver of sky between the bulldozer's arm and the joint of the scoop, but he doesn't really need to see. He already knows what will happen.

It starts with the lightning, a silent warning before the rupture. Next comes the thunder, only it's no ordinary rumble; this thunder splits a hole in the sky.

From the cloudy purple heavens, the crows emerge.

They move like a plague, their black wings billowing. Their cries peal away into the night, their sharp beaks pointed in the same direction, always.

He covers his head, even though he's protected under the bulldozer. It's more to deaden the sound.

When the crows finally pass, they leave in their wake a silence thick enough to blanket the entire forest, and this is when he hears the footsteps resume.

Closer. They're closer now.

He uncovers his ears to hear where they're coming from, but it seems to him they're coming from all sides of the clearing. Risking a peek, he peers into the dark, but the machinery makes grotesque silhouettes against the dim light of the purple sky. From where he hides, every crane looks like a gallows, every woodpile a crouching beast. Even the colorful tents laid out across the clearing look sinister, their garish carnival colors muted and transformed in the dark.

The spaces between the trees are what he's watching, though. Then he sees the first one emerge.

Run!

He keeps to the middle of the clearing, away from the dark

places, but he's exposed. His feet thunder against the soft earth, boots slipping over slick leaves and freshly unpacked dirt. He pumps his arms and pushes away the burning in his chest, the wheezing in his throat. He knows he's being followed, but he doesn't dare turn to see how closely.

Now that he's seen them, there's no way they'll let him go.

The clearing seems to stretch for miles, but when he finally reaches the back of it, he has no choice except to dive through the gaping maw of the forest again. He's forgotten how dense the vegetation is through here.

* * *

At last, he breaks through and runs headlong into a chain-link fence, the tower it guards looming over him like a metal giant. Signs all over the fence warn against trespassing, but if he still had a way in, he would risk it.

He runs along the fence, considering the time it would take to climb it.

The thought of going back in there . . .

But there's no time. Footfalls beat the ground behind him in a steady rhythm, and he quickens his sprint around the corner of the fence, bringing him to the back of the building.

Far in the distance, the whistle of the train blares, and he wishes it would stop because he can no longer hear the footfalls.

After another second, though, he understands that it isn't the train that's whistling. It's them . . . whistling to one another.

"Please don't!"

But his pleading won't be heard.

His hands drag along the fence now, groping for any hint of an opening. A fallen loop of barbed wire hooks the skin of his hand, and he pulls back like he's been bitten, droplets of blood splattering the grass underneath him.

His voice quavers. "Where is the door?"

It's around the third turn in the fencing, obscured behind a thick knot of overgrowth. He has to beat back the thought of being dragged into the forest, fingers clawing at the ground.

Not again.

"Come on, come on," he whispers, fumbling with the chain that's wrapped unsecured around the fence opening.

When he's loosened it enough to open the gate a crack, he squeezes through, tearing his shirt in the process. He slips through the door just as he hears the crack of a twig close by.

Inside it's cold and drafty, and even the sound of his breath echoes through the cavernous halls. He already knows there's no lock inside the door. All he can do is outrun them, so he feels his way along the walls.

"They didn't see me," he tries to reassure himself, but he doesn't believe it.

A nearby rattle alerts him to movement along the chain-link fence outside.

He opens his eyes wider through the dark, but the draft just makes them burn, and he forces his shaking legs to carry him farther into the dark building.

His shin catches the leg of a chair, and he stumbles, throwing the chair to the ground with a crash. He reaches for a lantern on the nearby table and brings out a gentle light.

He sprints now, arms in front of him as he tries to remember the places to hide. There used to be so many.

Just then, his elbow knocks against a doorway.

"Here," he breathes, then more excited. "Here!"

He feels along the opposite wall, the hiding place coming back to him now. With a hard push, the wall gives way, and then the floor drops out.

The fall is farther than he remembers, and for a moment, his vision goes black. When he tries to stand, his ankle falters under a fiery pain, and before he can catch himself, he cries out.

His voice ricochets, and he looks up at the opening in the floor above. He's so still, he thinks maybe he's forgotten how to move.

When no one appears in the opening, his breath slowly returns. Careful not to place too much weight on his ankle, he hobbles in a half circle, preparing to make his way out. He's safe now.

Then he finishes his turn.

"No . . . n-n-nooo!" he stammers, trying to back away from them, but his ankle collapses under him, and he falls to his knees, the perfect place from which to beg.

"I didn't see anything. I swear it. I'll never tell a soul," he says, but his voice, where is his voice? It's barely a whisper.

They'll let me go. They'll see I mean it, and they'll let me go.

But he already knows that's not true.

"Please," he manages to say once more before his throat unleashes a rabid scream.

Then the dark overtakes him.

CHAPTER 1

SIX MONTHS EARLIER

I'm supposed to be excited because I'll get my own room.

In Germany—in everywhere, really—Mya and I always had to share. This house has space to spare, though, or at least that's what Mom has said about a dozen times already.

She told us first when we were packing our bags and filling just a few cardboard boxes in our apartment, taping the tops hurriedly and labeling them with a fat black marker. She told us again while we crammed into our airplane seats, holding our backpacks and a whole lot of unanswered questions. She told us at every rest stop and motel across three more states until we finally made it to Raven Brooks, to a street called Friendly Court, to a big, rickety blue house where Dad grew up, which now belongs to us because Grandma and Grandpa are dead.

"There might even be space for a playroom!" Mom says wistfully as we roll into the driveway. Never mind that Mya and I are a little too old to be "playing" anymore. Mya still has toys, but these days, I'm more into drawing.

It's possible that Mom is so chatty about all the stuff we have to look forward to in our new home because Dad has been intermittently mute throughout our whole trip. One minute, he's full of his usual optimism, acting like a grown-up kid; the next minute, he disappears into a place none of us can see. My guess is wherever he keeps drifting off to is the place that answers all the questions about what we left behind in Germany, and how much of it has followed us here.

As we roll up the driveway beside the truck, I see one or two neighbors pop their heads out their front doors before retreating inside like groundhogs. By the time we've opened the back of the truck, nearly every house on the block is dotted with one or two neighbors, clutching bathrobes closed and tucking newspapers under their arms. Not a single person comes over to say hello. Not one of them raises a hand to wave.

"Is that my box? That's my box! Mom, that one's mine!" Mya squeaks from the driveway as the lone mover needed to move our meager possessions begins lugging boxes from the small truck. The dude looks grumpy, like he can't believe this is all we have, or maybe that's just me being defensive. Anyway, I can tell we're in his way, so I tug on the back of Mya's shirt.

"Mouse, let's go pick our rooms," I say.

"Dibs!" she yells, pushing past me to barrel through the front door.

"You can't call dibs; you don't even know what you're calling dibs *on*!" I say, chasing after her.

"Dibs on whichever room *you* want!" she calls over her shoulder, beating me to the front door.

"Hang on, hang on, hang on," I say, dropping to a squat to examine my ankle.

"What?" Mya crouches next to me to examine whatever it is I'm looking at.

"I think I just . . . *completely owned you*," I say, pushing her over and scrambling to the door.

She springs back up, and as I take my first step inside the house, I feel her foot loop around mine, and she sends me flying across the floor.

Now that we're both inside the house, looking for our rooms suddenly feels a lot less important.

I trace the outlines of the room we walk straight into, the foyer, more or less an afterthought as the house opens into a small family room, with a worn green sofa and a television stand already positioned. I halfway expect to see someone sitting in it, eating Chinese takeout from a box on a folding snack tray. I brush the shiver from my neck; the thought that the house hasn't been fully vacated yet isn't exactly a welcome one.

I turn around and see the kitchen directly behind us, a long table cutting through the middle of it, a pantry tucked into the wall, a hallway set apart from the stairwell that leads upstairs. I follow Mya as she wanders toward the farthest hallway and see that there's a separate set of stairs leading downward. Without a word, Mya and I both walk down before we consider traveling up.

The first room down the stairs is a laundry room, or at least it should be. The machines are missing, a giant outlet on the wall showing where they should be. On the left are a couple more empty rooms, and on the right, the first door resists, its wood warped against the frame. With a tug, it finally comes loose, and when I feel for a light switch, I find a flashlight in the corner instead, standing on its head. When I click it on, I see that the room isn't a room but a hallway leading farther into the depths of the house.

I turn to Mya. "You first."

"No, thanks."

I take a step into the darkness. The last room on the right is cluttered with furniture. A massive wooden desk takes up the majority of the stuffy room, but additional bookshelves, glass-doored cabinets, and unhung pictures line the walls of the room, not to mention about a half dozen mystery objects hidden under white sheets, because clearly this place needed some additional creep factor.

I'm now at least halfway sure we've crashed the wrong house. It's only the wood carving of a plaque on the wall commemorating Roger A. and Adelle R. Peterson that gives me more confidence this place actually did belong to the grandparents I never met and who Dad hardly ever talks about.

* * *

"Maybe they were spies," Mya says.

It's this game we started playing when we got on the plane for America: Guess the grandparent. We've speculated everything from ornithologists to ghost hunters. I think we both just assumed that once we arrived at their house, it would become clear what they were and why they've always been such a closely kept secret. So far, the only clue into who our dad's parents were is the picture hanging on the wall above the light switch: a man with a skinny tie and thick-rimmed glasses and a woman with hair wound up into a beehive. They have to be our grandparents. The way the man stands with his hands on the woman's shoulders looks exactly like how Dad holds Mom . . . or how he used to hold her.

"They look like they're in a lab," I say, staring at the picture.

"Scientists?" Mya said. Strangely, that line of work never occurred to us. What could be so secretive about science?

"Where are you guys?" Mom calls from somewhere above.

Mya and I trot down the hall and up the back stairs to find Mom standing in the living room staring at the same sofa I was just looking at a few minutes before.

"Wait until you see the study," I say to her, and she looks at me with equal parts humor and scorn.

"Well, I don't suppose it was the easiest job, getting rid of all of the furniture after . . ."

After they died. That's what she wants to say, but like everything since Germany, she's tiptoeing around whatever she means.

Dad walks through the door behind her, and the three of us turn to see what he'll do.

It's hard to say what I'm expecting. After all, this is the house he grew up in. But he didn't so much as blink when we drove underneath the iron archway welcoming us to the town of Raven Brooks, a place he says he hasn't been since he first left it after college. And he didn't say a word when we turned down Friendly Court and rolled up to the blue house alongside the moving truck. If Dad's going to react to anything, this is his last chance to do it.

Maybe I caught him flinch. It was so tiny, almost a twitch of his jaw. Aside from that, though, Dad hardly lets on that the house should be familiar, that his formative years took place right here in these rooms, between these walls. He's all business, quietly taking inventory of what furniture remains. When he finds Mya and me staring at him, he sets his face in a smile, ruffling my hair and tugging on Mya's ponytail before walking back outside to bring in more boxes.

Mom was waiting for something, too; I can tell. Maybe some guidance about how she should be feeling. When she doesn't get it, she turns to us, remembers her optimism, and says, "Have you picked your rooms yet?"

Mya switches gears a split second faster than me, and she's up the stairs and down the hall before I can catch her. Luckily, she wants the room with the pink walls. I like pink, but something tells me I'd feel like I was drowning in cough syrup every morning when I woke up. I snag the room facing the street instead, and I like that just fine. There's a tree that shades part of the room; when I open the window, I can practically touch the closest branch. There's a bland but cozy-looking turquoise house across the street. And, tucked into the corner of the room, there's already a desk with a nice flat surface for drawing.

I've just started imagining what I'll sketch first when a thin, high whine wafts through the room.

My first thought is of a baby doll. There was this toy shop downstairs from our apartment in Germany that sold old novelties like jack-in-the-boxes and pinwheels. There was a doll with a string in the back of it that cried when you pulled it. Sometimes on warm nights when we had our windows open, I'd swear I could hear that weird doll crying in the distance, even though the shop was closed.

It's weird how you can forget where you are so fast. But sounds can do that, and this sound brings me right back to our apartment.

Then, as quietly as it drifts toward me, the high whine drifts away, leaving behind a stillness in my new room that unnerves me.

When Mya pokes her head through the doorway, I jump enough to make her notice.

"Cripes, Mya! Wear a bell or something, would you?"

"I wouldn't have to if you weren't such a . . ."

She tucks her fists under her armpits and flaps her arms slowly, holding eye contact.

"Oh, you're *dead*," I say, launching after her, and we nearly flatten the mover on the stairs who's just trying to do his job.

* * *

All day I try to act normal, and I get the sense everyone else is trying, too. Dad cracks jokes about claiming his old room back (the bedroom I chose—complete with bunkbeds); Mya unpacks my lockpick set before my parents can see it and slips it to me behind her back; Mom hums and twirls around the kitchen while she puts coffee mugs into cupboards, retracing the steps to an old dance routine I remember she used to perform at Fernweh Welt, the last amusement park my dad designed.

It's great that we're all trying, but if I look too closely at Dad's eyes, I can see the way he's looking past me at this house that used to be his and suddenly is again. I can feel Mya's hand trembling as she palms me my leather case of lockpicks. I can hear Mom's humming falter the tiniest bit when she sings that old, familiar tune that used to pipe through the speakers of the performance stage.

When I can't take all the trying anymore, I find myself in the basement—a little escape in this big house—and shut out the effort of it all. I just want to silence the questions piling up in my brain.

What happened after that day at the park?

What exactly did we leave behind in Germany?

Is this really our new home?

Why doesn't Dad ever talk about Raven Brooks? About my grandparents?

It's these questions and so many more that keep my hand frozen over a stack of blank paper, a red pencil primed and ready to go.

The basement is pretty dreary—windowless, with nothing more than a hanging light bulb here and there.

I try holding a few sheets of paper up to the walls, but then an idea strikes me.

I bound back up the basement stairs.

"Mom, I need some boards," I say to her as she seeks out a drawer to put the knives in. When she turns, she's holding a particularly menacing-looking butcher knife.

"On second thought, maybe I'll just find them on my own," I say, and she looks confused for a minute. Then she turns to see the knife in her hand.

"What was it you said you needed?"

"Boards," I say. "Like, wooden planks or something."

Mom looks tired. She puts the heel of her hand to her forehead and closes her eyes.

"Should I even ask why?"

I shake my head.

"I thought I saw some tools in the backyard, maybe near that old potting shed. You're welcome to whatever you can find," she says.

I run out the front door and barely dodge the mover carrying in a heavy box of machine parts. A lone white arm dangles from the box, its robotic joints dormant and unprogrammed.

"Watch for spiders! Or snakes! Or whatever else breeds here!" Mom calls out, remembering to worry.

"Yup!"

I spot the splintering potting shed in a far corner of the overgrown backyard, but all that stands against the side of it is a dirt-caked shovel and a rusted screwdriver. Just my luck; the door to the shed is padlocked shut.

I glance stealthily over my shoulder to make sure I'm alone before sliding the leather lockpick pouch from my pocket.

It wasn't a skill I intended to pick up, not really. It's just that there was a lot to explore in Germany. A *lot*. Our apartment building alone was over two hundred years old, and our landlord wasn't exactly the sharing type. He forbade Mya and me from rummaging in the most interesting places, like closed-off basements and attic storage spaces. The lockpick set was for sale at a local traveling market, and it seemed like too much of a coincidence that it could have been right there, on sale for the exact amount of Deutsche Mark I had in my pocket, on the exact day Mr. Fischer had chased us off from the basement door.

"We could wait until after dark," I remember telling Mya, who had nodded earnestly. That very night, in the basement of our two-hundred-year-old apartment building, I fumbled my way through all the picks, trying to remember what the salesman had told me while Mya held the flashlight steady. When we finally got in, the basement turned out to be a total bust—just some dusty old dressers, some old lanterns, and a bicycle. That really wasn't the point, though; the opened lock was. Suddenly, I had a master key to an entire world of secrets . . . or at least I would as soon as I got better at picking.

I guess I never really thought of it as wrong. There are people who can decipher codes, people who can translate languages. I can pop locks.

I realize, though, that not everyone sees it this way, which is why I'd rather not get caught. It's not that I'd get into trouble for busting into a rickety potting shed. It's that Mya's the only one who knows my secret skill, and I'd rather keep it that way.

The padlock is an easy one, but it's rusted, so I have to chisel the gunk away first. After that, the lock is on the ground in three seconds, and inside the shed, I find a ton of spiderwebs, a few sheets of plywood, and some dusty cans of paint that I assume were left over from painting the outside of the house about a thousand years ago.

"Jackpot."

I drag the boards from the shed along with a few of the small buckets of paint. All that's left are the brushes, and after absolutely not screaming when a spider crawls down my arm from one of the bristles, I emerge from the shed with what I need.

"Honey, pick those up! You're going to carve a line right across the floor. Oh for Pete's sake, Aaron!"

Mom is still scolding me when I reach the basement stairs, bumping the plywood on each step as I descend.

I decide I'm going to be surrounded by sunlight. Sunny days never seem to stay long enough, but I can fix that. Down here, I can sit under the sun and draw no matter what's going on up there. Down here, it'll be okay.

I paint the sun a bright yellow. It's the bucket with the least amount of paint in it, but I make it go as far as I can. When I finally do run out, I switch to blue and make sure the sky covers most of the wood that remains. I don't have any more colors, so I mix the blue into the empty yellow bucket and let it absorb the color from the bottom and the sides until green emerges, and at the bottom of the pictures, I draw hills of grass.

Later that night, after the paint has dried, I take one of the thick black markers we used to label our moving boxes and draw a perfect + across the pictures, framing them into four equal window panes. I prop the boards against the walls and stand back to examine my work. The single light bulb above does its best to illuminate the room, and my paintings still manage to cast brightness into the basement.

Down here, no one can see in; it doesn't matter what my family's done. I can simply *be*.

I'm just about to turn off the light and head up to dinner when I hear the basement door open. Mya pads down the stairs in her socks with the little rubber grips on the bottoms. They make a peeling sound each time she steps.

"I don't want to go to sleep tonight," she says, sitting in front of the paintings. She doesn't need to say she likes them. She's already sitting under them, so they're doing exactly what they're supposed to do.

"What's the matter?" I say, sitting beside her.

"I had a nightmare last night," she says. She's matter-of-fact, but she's scared.

"I know," I tell her.

My parents were in the adjoining motel room with their door cracked, but if either of them woke when Mya started thrashing, they didn't let on. I rolled from my bed and sat on the edge of hers, putting my hand in hers and letting her squeeze so hard it hurt, but it was one of the only things that settled her down when she had one of her nightmares. She never really wakes from them. She just sort of drifts away again, going to wherever she goes that isn't as scary.

She used to get night terrors once in a while when she was younger, but I'd never seen it so bad as when we were in Germany. Especially after the accident. Since then, it's been almost every night.

"So, you're just going to stay awake forever?" I say, staring at the sunny sky I've created.

"I think so, yeah."

"Might get a little boring."

She thinks for a minute. "I'll learn Mandarin."

I nod approvingly. "Ambitious."

"Do you think anyone is looking . . . for us?" she asks after a while.

I shake my head automatically, even though I've asked myself that same question at least a hundred times and have yet to come up with an answer. I'm trying not to be angry that I can't ask Mom or Dad, because why bother? They'll only get all weird and evasive and change the subject, or Dad will fall into one of his bad moods, and it's just not worth it.

So instead, I keep shaking my head and saying, "Nah." And when that doesn't feel like enough, I say, "Definitely not."

She doesn't say anything, so I'm not sure if that means she believes me and feels better or knows I'm lying and doesn't want to hear me lie more. Maybe I'm just like Mom and Dad to her.

"Dinner! Where are you two?" I hear Mom say from upstairs. She sounds tired. Her voice always gets higher when she's tired.

Mya and I hustle up the steps so we don't make things worse by dawdling. When we stumble into the kitchen, the table is set, and Dad is already a huge presence. Something has changed between this morning and now, when it's just the four of us, and we're left to look at one another across the table over takeout boxes.

"I haven't unpacked the dishes yet," Mom says by way of apologizing for the food we'd always rather eat anyway. Maybe she's saying it for Dad's sake. He stares at the flattened hamburger in its little Styrofoam box, a bundle of limp french fries beside it on a plastic place mat.

"Where have you two been?" he asks, his voice quiet. He doesn't look up.

Mya looks at me.

"The basement," I say.

"Why?" he says, and it doesn't feel like there's a right answer.

"Just . . . exploring," I say.

"Don't you have enough to do in your room? You have your own rooms now," he grumbles, slowly picking up his burger.

Okay, so there was the right answer. I should have said *enjoying my new room.*

"Yeah," I say, lowering myself into my chair. Mya follows. Mom lifts her eyebrows at me, trying to urge me to say something more, but it feels like I'm tiptoeing through a minefield. This is what it's like now with Dad. It's so good until it goes bad. Then we're all . . . wrong.

"Um, it's cool," I say, and Dad finally looks up, suspicious. "The room," I clarify.

He keeps staring at me.

"Thank you?" I try.

"Is that a question?" he says, squeezing the ketchup out of his burger. I watch it drip onto the to-go container.

"I like mine, too," Mya chimes in, and immediately his expression softens. Not much, but enough. He's always gentler with Mya.

Mom releases a quiet breath I didn't realize she'd been holding, and we all chew in silence. It's at least better than facing the inquisition.

"Didn't that used to be your mother's sewing room?" Mom

says, finally taking a bite of her own burger. "Mya's room, I mean?"

Dad starts chewing more slowly. "Mmhmm."

"I thought that's what I remember you saying," Mom says, her voice trailing off toward the end.

"Did Grandma sew a lot?" Mya asks, first directing her question toward Dad, but when he doesn't answer, she looks to Mom.

"Not sure she had time for that," Mom says, choosing her words carefully as she eyes Dad. He's back to focusing on the placemat.

"No, she didn't," he says, like that answers anything at all. I'm trying so hard not to be mad about leaving, about having to move here basically in the middle of the night, about Dad's scary moods, but it's all getting hard, and he makes it harder when he stops talking altogether. And what's so wrong with telling your kids about their grandparents anyway? Shouldn't he want to share all these boring stories?

Mya looks from Mom to Dad for answers, and Mom finally speaks up.

"Grandma and Grandpa both worked very hard," she says, and Dad's grip on his burger tightens.

"Doing what?" says Mya. I can't tell if she's being oblivious or just pushing her luck.

"They were scientists," Mom says carefully, but now I'm hoping Mya keeps pushing because this is starting to get interesting.

"You mean like, doctors, or—?"

"Something like that," Mom says, starting to squirm.

Then Mya looks at me, mischief glittering in her eyes. "Like *mad* scientists?" she says, and I have to pick it up now because she's practically lobbed the ball into my court.

"Like evil geniuses," I say, and we both start in with our best evil laughs, and Mom looks like she's about to pop.

Not before Dad does, though.

"Enough!" he roars suddenly, standing hard enough to hit the dining room table and then bending to clutch his kneecap.

Mom practically chokes on her burger, and Mya and I stare at each other because that's the safest place to look. We should have known this was going to happen.

"Ted," Mom tries after she's managed to swallow her bite. "Come on."

This is the way Mom talks to him now, like she's measuring the balance between asking and pleading. This never used to be Mom.

Dad looks around like he can't remember why he's angry. That doesn't stop him from crumpling his paper napkin into a tight ball and throwing it onto the table, pivoting on his heel to leave the room.

"Where are you going?" Mom asks, now actually sounding worried.

"Meeting Ike," he says without turning. Instead, he strides over to the living room and shoves his feet into his shoes.

"This late?"

"He *works* late," Dad says, and he finally sounds like he's calming down a little. He turns to Mom.

"Security guard work," he says, and the look on his face is an apology.

Mom accepts it by saying nothing.

Then, without another word, Dad opens the front door of the house he grew up in and leaves like it's just any other house in the world.

CHAPTER 2

Such a big decision. Will it be the blue shirt with yellow stripes or the yellow shirt with blue stripes?

It would probably make Mom sad to know how little I care about what I wear on my first day of school in Raven Brooks. She made a special trip all the way to the outlet malls just so she could get Mya and me clothes we'd feel comfortable in. She's trying, I know she is.

Dad is, too. This morning he pulled out a waffle maker that hasn't seen the light of day for at least a year. He had to plug it into a converter since he first bought it in Germany, which meant he had to detach the power drill he was trying to charge, only to discover we didn't have any vanilla, so he gave us extra syrup to make up for it.

"Can't have you guys going hungry on your first day," he'd said while he filled every single square with butter and maple.

It's not that we aren't grateful. I can tell Mya is smiling even harder than normal so our parents can't see how nervous she is. And I'm smiling—a step up from basically never smiling—because I don't want them to know how *not* nervous I am, even though I probably should be.

It's just that school feels really unimportant in light of every-thing else that happened this summer. And it's hard to feel like this isn't all just temporary anyway. At least half of me is expecting to wake up any day now and find out we're leaving, even though we just got here. I've pictured it more times than I can count: Dad nudging me awake, an empty cardboard box in his hands, "How docs London sound?" Or Mom whispering in my ear, "Hurry now, we leave for Ontario tomorrow."

We left Germany in a hurry, so why not leave Raven Brooks just as fast?

Apparently, though, we're staying long enough to have to attend school, at least for now, so I have to choose a striped shirt I don't care about and a pair of shorts I don't care about and go to class and learn about things I don't care about. All while I wait to see when and where we'll go next.

"Yellow with the blue stripes," Mya says from behind me.

I turn to see her wearing her own new first-day outfit: frayed denim shorts, green shirt knotted to the side, and the plastic purple watch she never takes off.

"You don't look like an ogre," I say.

"Thanks," she says. "You still do, but I'm sure you'll be forgiven."

"Why are we even bothering with this?" I ask her.

"You mean school?"

"I mean pretending we aren't . . . temporary."

"I dunno," Mya says, staring at a spot on the carpet. "I'm starting to think this is where we're staying."

I watch her closely, trying to break her code. I know Mya better than anyone, and even I have a hard time reading her sometimes.

"This place is weird," I say.

"You've barely even left the house," Mya says, straightening her ponytail.

"Well, this house is weird," I say.

"Aaron," she says, finally looking at me, "*we're* weird. Face it, we are home."

Little sisters aren't supposed to be right as often as Mya is, and it's times like these when it annoys me the most.

"You have syrup on your shirt," I say, because at the moment, that's my leg up. Pathetic. Then I drag my backpack down the stairs, hitting every step with a bump.

Mom gives me a kiss on the top of my head. "Where's your sister?"

"Syrup," I say, then move on to my dad.

He takes my shoulders in his burly hands. It would have been so easy for him to be disappointed in me. Physically, he's everything I'm not: wide-shouldered, with limbs that could be trained to swing heavy bats or throw balls fast and far. The only thing I've ever been good at—or had any interest in doing—is wielding a colored pencil.

And Dad is proud of me. He tells me so, and he means it, too. He doesn't mean everything he says, but about that, he's telling the truth. He says I "have an eye," then I tell him I have two, and he laughs and I laugh, and it's been thousands of moments strung together just like that. And that's all we need to say because we both know how talking about it can kill it, so we let it be.

"Go draw the world on fire," he says.

I nod. This is what we say instead. Instead of *Go light the world on fire*, he tells me to draw it. I'm pretty sure he thinks drawing is what keeps me away from the same boundless mania that consumes him when he works. He has no idea I inherited it from him, and that both come from the same place inside me.

Mya finally skips down the stairs, a tiny wet spot on her shirt where the syrup used to be.

We walked to the schools the other day so we'd know how to get there. Conveniently, the elementary, middle, and high schools are all lined up next to one another.

Friendly Court is so quiet, I wonder for a moment if all those people who were watching us move in were hired extras, and this is some sort of huge joke nobody's let us in on yet. But as soon as we round the corner onto Third Street, I see a few more kids with backpacks, and I decide maybe there just aren't any other kids on our block. Sometimes, the easiest answer wins out.

Mya and I are nearly silent as we walk side by side, which makes hearing the two kids behind us so easy.

"How do you get this far in life and not know the difference between a mule and a donkey?" says a girl.

"I do know the difference, and it was one thousand percent a donkey," says a guy.

"Bet me a sandwich," the girl says.

A pause.

"A sandwich?"

"Yeah. I like sandwiches. You know that. Much better than you know the difference between a mule and a donkey," she says.

I have to turn and look. I really have no choice. I didn't realize Mya had already turned to stare.

"Hey, settle this for us," says a tall, skinny kid with braces and a mess of dark, curly hair. The girl next to him is much smaller, but she's got to be about Mya's age by the way she talks.

"Um, okay," I say, because really, what else am I gonna say?

"Donkeys versus mules," says the girl, and I'm confused. Is this a question?

"Like, who would win in a battle, or—?"

The girl rolls her eyes. "Obviously, it would be a mule. That's not what I mean, though."

"The difference between them?" Mya tries.

The girl looks at my sister like she's finally found another smart person.

"Yes! Thank you," she says.

"They aren't the same thing?" I say before I mean to. The three of them look at me like I'm bringing down the human race or something.

"Mules are a mix between a donkey and a horse," says Mya. "Donkeys are just . . . donkeys."

"Right," says the girl, looking at the boy who's probably my age. "Which means mules look more like horses. They're bigger because they're part horse. It was a mule."

The boy clenches his jaw as he debates. The girl hops a little victory hop, clasping her hands together.

"Oooh, I see a sandwich in my future!"

Then she looks at my sister. "I'm Maritza," she says, now that the great donkey/mule debate is settled.

My sister waves back. "Mya. This is my brother, Aaron."

The girl smiles and rolls her eyes, grabbing Mya's arm and pushing ahead of us. "Aren't brothers great?"

Mya looks back at me for a second before letting the girl pull her away.

"Enzo," says the guy. "My sister's annoying."

"I have one of those," I say, and hey, maybe I've made my first friend since moving here.

"We just moved into my gran—um, a house . . . on Friendly Court," I say. I don't know why, but it feels too soon to be telling people we're living in my grandparents' old house. I don't know, maybe it was something about the way people stared when we were unloading the truck.

"Friendly Court," says Enzo, looking up like he's trying to place the street.

I point behind us. "Right over there," I say.

"Oh! One of the old streets," he says, and immediately, I feel like he's socked me in the stomach. Okay, maybe I *haven't* found a friend.

He seems to pick up on what I'm thinking, though, because he looks down at the sidewalk while he walks. "I didn't mean it in a bad way," he says. "That's just what people call it. It . . . it doesn't mean anything, you know?"

He means it doesn't mean we're worse than the people who live in the newer houses.

"Oh," I say, not sure I want to let him off the hook yet, but one more sidelong look at Enzo makes me think he's not a bad guy. Maybe he just doesn't think before he opens his mouth all the time.

In fact, I'm not sure Enzo could lob an insult even if he was trying to. There's a sort of dopey smile all over him, not just on his face, but in everything he does: the way he takes big strides with his even bigger feet, or the way he swings his arms while he walks, or how his nose whistles when he breathes because he tries to keep his mouth shut over his braces. The weirdest thing, though, is that he doesn't try to hide any of it. If Enzo is aware that he's not the coolest, he doesn't seem to care. There's a certain kind of relief that comes with being around a person like that; like for once, I can take a deep breath and let my face and my body do whatever they're going to do, and who cares if someone is watching?

"By the way, and I'm just putting this out there," says Enzo, "if you've seen the new *SpaceKills* movie, don't tell me anything. Like five people have almost spoiled the ending for me, and I'm totally on edge."

It's so random. It's so perfect.

"Dude, I thought I was the last person in the world who hadn't seen it yet," I say.

His eyes widen. "The way they left the last movie, I swear I don't know how it could get any more gruesome than that."

"Here's hoping they find a way. I heard they almost had to pass out barf bags in the theaters."

We both stand for a moment, lost in thought, before continuing the walk to school.

The campus looks completely different now that it's swarming with sweating kids who all look about as lost as me, which automatically makes me feel a little bit better. Maybe this won't be so bad after all.

Mya and Maritza split off toward the elementary school, and I give Mya an almost imperceptible nod, but she catches it and nods back, so she knows I won't be far in case anything goes south.

"What've you got first?" Enzo says, peering over my shoulder at my schedule. "Oh, Mr. Davni. He's cool. Just don't touch the toy collection on his desk. He's weird about that."

I register the warning.

"How about Mrs. Levy? I have her for Biology."

"Strict," he says. "I heard she kicked a kid out of class for having hiccups. Turns out he had this condition. They didn't go away for three months. She still failed him, though."

"Whoa. What about Tierney for Algebra?"

"He hates grading, so basically, you do all your homework in class while he comes around and checks it."

"That sounds great," I say.

"Yeah, except he eats a ton of garlic. I mean like inhuman amounts. How long can you hold your breath for?"

"I've never timed it," I say.

"You'll get good. Okay, who else?"

"Ryland for Geography."

"Obsessed with earthquakes. You'll basically be learning about fault lines for the entire year."

"Delvy for History," I say.

"Hates Ryland."

"Oh."

"Don't worry. It only ever comes up when we do Class Battles, and that's not until midway through the year." He leans in conspiratorially. "It's like my dad says: all politics."

Interesting. Not a problem I was expecting in middle school.

"Oh, hey, you have Donaldson for Civics. Me too! We'll be in final period together."

"Cool," I say. Honestly, more than being in the same class as him, I'm relieved that *he* seems excited about it.

"I probably better go find my locker. It always takes me about a million tries to get the combination right," he says, and there he goes again, openly admitting he's pure dork. I'm baffled. Also, I'm jealous.

Then, suddenly, I watch him fall apart, piece by piece, right there in front of me.

He starts to quake so hard, I can actually see him vibrating from where I'm standing. Sweat breaks out on the back of his neck so fast, I think at first that it must have started raining inexplicably. But nope, that's classic nervous sweating, and if that wasn't enough, the distinct shade of red his cheeks have turned would have been a dead giveaway.

He swallows audibly.

I look past him to find a tallish girl with dark brown skin and sparkling brown eyes approach us with complete ease. If she's aware that she's just destroyed my new friend with barely a glance in his direction, she doesn't acknowledge it.

"Did you see Kornwell's teaching Study Skills instead of Chemistry this year?" she says, diving right in like she's picking up a stray conversation.

She turns to me like we already know each other. "He tried to shrink a rabbit last year," she says to me. It's a lot to process.

"Wait . . . what?"

"Exactly," she says, smiling, and I'm starting to understand why Enzo is a useless pool of sweat and babble next to me. It's sort of hard not to be charmed by her.

"He claimed to have the chemical composition for a shrinking formula figured out, so he 'borrowed' Mrs. Neederman's class bunny, but all the chemical did was make the rabbit smell like rotten eggs, and then it got loose and made its way into the ventilation ducts. It hid for three days before they could find it, and the entire school smelled like sewage until they did."

"That can't be real," I say.

"I couldn't get the smell out of my nose for a week," she says. "Anyway, now Mr. Kornwell is teaching Study Skills, which is basically where kids go to take after-lunch naps," she says. "Hi, I'm Trinity."

"Hey. Aaron," I say.

"Blurbum," says Enzo.

We turn to him.

"Bu—blurb—um . . ."

What is happening?

"Okay," says Trinity, entirely unfazed. "Gotta get to first period. Nice meeting you," she says to me, then smiles at Enzo like he didn't just say "blurbum."

"That was . . . I've never seen a meltdown like that," I say to Enzo.

"She's magical. I have no control over it," he says, recovering faster than I expect him to.

"How long have you known her?"

"Three hundred and sixty-eight days," he says.

"And you still haven't said—?"

"Not a word."

"Wow."

"It almost feels like I can't break the streak now," he says. "What would I even say?"

"I mean, you could start with 'Hi, Trinity' and go from there," I say. "Just a thought."

He considers this. "It could work."

He's an absolute mess. Definitely my friend.

* * *

The day goes reasonably well, and I guess somewhere along the way, I became a pessimist, because I'm actually surprised. But glad-surprised.

Mr. Davni is absolutely weird about his desk toys. Our first ten minutes of class were devoted to all the consequences for touching them, playing with them, stealing them, even staring at them for too long. Mrs. Levy is strict, and it seems like she's got an especially short fuse for bodily functions. A girl next to me coughed, and I watched Mrs. Levy wipe an actual chill from her arm. Mr. Tierney is cool, and it turns out I can hold my breath for eight seconds, ten if I really push it. Any more than that, I'll definitely pass out, so I just need to time my work right so when he comes around, I only need help with an easy problem to explain. Mrs. Ryland believes The Big One is coming any day. She described her home earthquake preparedness kit, showed us where the classroom kit is, and even told us she keeps a kit in her car. Nobody brings up the fact that we don't even live near a fault line. And Mr. Delvy for sure hates Mrs. Ryland. Classroom Battles didn't even come up (whatever that is), but he still managed to get a dig in about "kooky Mrs. Quakes."

By the time I get to Mr. Donaldson's class for Civics, a class we share with the grade above us, I almost have myself convinced that it won't be so bad starting over in Raven Brooks. Maybe it could be this easy to fall into a place and not worry about how you land.

"Over here," says Enzo, waving to me the minute I walk through the door. He's grabbed us seats front and center. Not usually my style, but I'm grateful to see a familiar face, especially after practically short-circuiting during lunchtime when I realized I didn't know where I was going to sit, so I ended up on the edge of a planter box outside.

"So?" he says.

"You prepped me well," I say.

"Was I right about the toys?"

"Seriously, what's that all about?"

"I don't know, but I haven't met anyone who was willing to risk their hand to find out," says Enzo.

Trinity walks in, and immediately, he starts in with his disintegrating act.

So, I try to repay him for being so cool to me and call her over. That was apparently the wrong move.

"What are you *doing*?" he says.

"Say it with me: 'Hi, Trinity,'" I say.

"I'm not sure I like you anymore," he hisses, and Trinity sits down right beside him in the front row. I'm behind Enzo, so I can see the sweat starting to form on his neck already.

I scrawl him a note on my pad of paper and slide it under the desk to his left.

The back of his neck tenses, and he takes his giant foot and kicks me like a mule. Or a donkey? Anyway, he hits me right in the shin.

"Dude!"

Mr. Donaldson walks through the door like he's had just about all he can take for the day.

"Sit!" he grumbles, even though everyone is already seated.

"I'm Mr. Donaldson," he says like he's said it a million times already, like he hates his name, and he hates everyone. Still, there's something about this guy I like.

"Hello, sir," says the class with the perfect level of sarcasm.

Well, *most* of the class says that. Everyone, in fact, except for the tall kid in the front row who's sweating hard enough to flood the room. He says "Hi, Trinity."

If her name had only been one syllable, the fumble might have been drowned out by the rest of the class's voices. But no, Trinity is three syllables, and everyone—*everyone*—heard Enzo finally say his first actual words to her.

I may have just lost my only friend.

"Actually, that's a good idea," Mr. Donaldson says, and at first I think he's going to embarrass Enzo even worse, but he decides to embarrass us all instead, one by one.

"Since this class has students from different grades, let's go around the room and introduce ourselves."

Low-level groans.

"Oh, I know, it's terrible. You actually have to act like sociable young people instead of animals in pants. Poor you."

Whoa. There's cynical, and then there's what I've heard Mom refer to as "clinically jaded." I think that's Mr. Donaldson.

We go down the rows, telling the class and a stony-faced Mr. Donaldson our first and last names, and on the bright side, this is less time we have to spend going over class rules and a syllabus that will be followed for half the year before it's discarded because nobody's doing the homework on time and everyone is confused.

"Enzo Esposito," says Enzo when it's his turn, and when he shifts in his chair, I can see that his notepad is sitting in his lap, and so help me the poor kid has actually written his own name so he was sure to get it right this time. I would laugh if I didn't feel like I was partly to blame.

"Young man?" says Mr. Donaldson, and at first I think he's talking to Enzo before I look up to find his eyes on me, eyebrows lifted in mild expectation.

"Me?"

"Yes. That's what we're doing here. You might have noticed a theme," he says.

Jeez.

"Um, Aaron," I say.

Mr. Donaldson closes his eyes like his head hurts. Trinity turns and mouths, *last name.*

"Oh, Aaron Peterson," I say.

Mr. Donaldson wakes up. In fact, his eyes are wider than they've been since he walked into the classroom looking like he wanted to walk right out.

"Peterson?" he says.

I've done something wrong. It's not my name. I'm still talking. I forgot to wear pants.

But no, none of that seems to be true.

It seems I'm not the only one confused. The rest of the class is taking turns staring at me, then staring at Mr. Donaldson, then at me again.

"Any relation to Roger and Adelle Peterson?" he says.

Thirty pairs of eyes fix on some part of me: my face, my back, my hands. Thirty pairs of eyes are looking for an answer to this question. And apparently, that answer means something.

"They're uh—*were*—they were my grandparents," I say. Weirdly, it's the first time I've said that aloud.

Mr. Donaldson cocks his head while his eyes peel through me. "Interesting."

"Is it?"

I didn't mean to say that part. It just sort of slipped out.

Now Mr. Donaldson looks as lost as I do.

"Wait, that's where you live? In the blue house on Friendly Court?" says Enzo, turning around in his seat. If he was trying to get me back for "helping" him talk to Trinity, bravo. Really, well done. Now everyone isn't just staring. They're whispering.

"Your grandparents were geniuses," says Mr. Donaldson above the murmurs. Somehow, it doesn't come out like a compliment.

"Okay," I say. What do you even say to something like that?

"Your, uh . . . your parents go into the family business?" Mr. Donaldson asks. How is it my eighth-period Civics teacher knows more about my grandparents' professions than I do? And why does he sound so . . . what? Suspicious? Concerned?

Is that *fear*?

I look slowly around the room for clues on the other kids' faces, but every time one of them catches me looking, they clam up and cast their eyes down.

I turn back to Mr. Donaldson. "I don't think so."

It's the most honest answer I can give, and it seems to both satisfy and disappoint him.

Then, just when I think the interrogation is almost over, a kid with stiff hair and a peeling sunburn who introduced himself as Seth Jenkins chimes in.

"I didn't know being the town wingnuts was a family business," he says, and the ripple of laughter through the class is enough to a) tell me what all the whispering was about, and b) make me wonder if I could fold a paper airplane sharp enough to pierce Seth Jenkins's skull.

Mr. Donaldson's already on it, though.

"I think the word you're looking for is 'geniuses,' Mr. Jenkins, but I suspect that's not a word you come across too often."

Some kids start to laugh, but Mr. Donaldson puts a stop to that, too. "Roger and Adelle Peterson's advancements in geology and meteorology are still being studied at the university to this day. Their theories were way ahead of their time."

Then he turns to me, his expression impossible to read. "Your grandparents left behind quite a legacy."

I suppose I should say thank you. It almost sounds like a compliment. *Almost.*

* * *

Even if it was supposed to be praise, the last thing I want to do is thank Mr. Donaldson for bringing any of this up in front of the whole class. People seem to want to know where we came from, why we're here, who we are—all questions that sound like they're meant to be polite—but they're really trying to weed out the weirdos.

If Raven Brooks knew who we were, where we came from, why we were here . . . they'd expel us faster than you can say *wingnut*.

Now I have Mr. Donaldson giving people a whole new reason to look more closely at that family who moved into *that* blue house on *that* street where *those* people used to live.

I have virtually no memory of what happened during the rest of eighth period. I think I wrote my name in the corner of a textbook. I think I slid a syllabus into the front flap of a folder marked CIVICS. I think I wrote down a homework assignment that's due at the beginning of next week. All I know for sure is that I've made it outside into the muggy afternoon, and I've loaded my bag down with books I'll probably forget at home more often than not, and I've pretended not to hear Enzo call to me from across the courtyard because all I want to do is grab Mya and get home before I can see one more question form on the mouth of one more person who wants to know one more thing about me that I can't or won't tell them.

Mya's the first one out the front doors of the elementary school.

"Let's roll," I say, grabbing the strap of her backpack.

"I want to walk home with Maritza," she says, looking for her new friend.

"Not today," I say, and she starts to protest, but she must see the concern on my face somehow because she gives it up pretty easily and lets me pull her down the street and around the first corner we find, hopefully evading anyone for at least most of the walk home.

When we do finally walk through the door, our ankles are itchy from being scratched by alleyways full of overgrown weeds.

"How was the first day?" Dad asks the second we walk through the door. I didn't expect him to be right there. I didn't have a chance to fix my face into something resembling "meh."

"It was all right," I say with a shrug, but he's definitely not convinced. He looks to Mya for a more complete answer.

"I made a friend. Her name is Maritza, and she lives in New Town. And she's into mechanics and how things work, oh and she likes pie. And I like pie!"

"Wait a minute," Dad says, looking extremely serious.

He leans down, towering over Mya like a stone wall, his hands on his knees, his shoulders hunched. He fixes his green eyes on Mya's, and she looks right back, fearless.

"Did you say . . . she likes pie, too?"

"Uh-huh." Mya smiles.

"And—and you like pie?"

"Dad, you know I like pie."

Dad stands, pulling at the curly tip of his mustache while he contemplates this remarkable revelation.

Suddenly, he slaps the sides of his legs. "Well, I can see no way around it. You and Mitzy—"

"Maritza," she says.

"You and Maritza will simply have to be friends."

"Agreed," Mya says, and they share a stout handshake, one pump before letting go.

"You two are weird," I say.

49

Dad turns his sparkling eyes on me, and for just a second, today didn't happen. Raven Brooks didn't happen. Germany didn't happen.

For just a second, there isn't a single secret to hold or carry, and we're just the Petersons, four weirdos with a few geniuses sprinkled in, with no family legacy and nothing to whisper about and a dad whose job is so boring, it's not even worth talking about.

"And you?" he says. "Anyone there as interesting as you?"

It was the highest compliment to give in our very strange family, to be interesting.

"Maybe," I say, thinking Enzo probably qualifies. "I mean, not anyone interesting like *you*, but . . ."

Dad eyes me closely, then smiles like he always does when I skirt that line between funny and what Mom calls "smart."

He reaches out and puts his big hands on my shoulders, his forehead to my forehead.

"My son, my progeny, my heir-apparent . . ."

I wait. We stare.

"You will never—and I do mean never—find someone as interesting as me."

Then he laughs his earthquake-level laugh, the one that shakes his stomach and splits my eardrums in half. It's worth it, though. It's a great laugh.

I head upstairs to drop my bag and my notebooks in my room, but the sight of Mom sitting on her bed stops me. She's staring off into the distance, like something from another lifetime is haunting her, and she has zero idea I am watching her relive all of it behind her. The reflection of her face in the vanity mirror is so pale, I wonder at first if she's really even there, or if I'm seeing a ghost that resembles her.

I try to say something, but just as I open my mouth to ask if she's okay, she takes a big, slow breath, and as she lets it out, she says, "It will be different this time."

But nothing in the way she says it, nothing in the way her body sits rigid on the edge of the bed, says that she believes what she's telling herself.

"Mom?"

She doesn't turn at first, and I look behind me to see if Mya's following up the stairs, but I can hear her in the background, chattering away with Dad in the living room.

I try again, this time after taking a step into her room. "Mom?"

She slowly places her hands on the tops of her thighs, looks down at them, then looks up and turns to me. For just a second, it's like she's never seen me before.

Then she says, "Aaron? How long have you been standing there?"

"Just for a minute," I say, thinking I've done something wrong, though I have no idea what could be so wrong about looking at my mom while she talks to herself.

"I'm home from school," I say to her. It sounds so dumb coming out of my mouth, but it's almost like she needs a reminder about where I've been, or maybe where she is right now. I've never seen my mom act like this before.

Then, with one slow blink of her eyes, she's back.

"How was your day, hon?"

She smiles, and it's her usual smile, her same comforting glow, her same soft eyes. I've tried drawing her tons of times, but pencils and paint never seem to capture what she actually looks like.

"Mom?" I say. It's not the right time, but the right time doesn't really exist. Still, it doesn't come out like a question. "Everyone here knows who Grandma and Grandpa were, don't they?"

Her face is so still, I think maybe she's blinked back to her other self, the one that was there when I first came upstairs. But she turns her head away from me while she resets the expression on her face. When she turns back again, she's smiling. But I think she forgot that the vanity mirror is in front of her, and I could see her face change. And in that moment when her face changed, I saw her deciding how she wanted me to see her.

"They were very . . . influential," she says. She takes the same pause that everyone seems to take before they describe my grandparents. But these were Dad's *parents*, her in-laws. They were her family, too. What could be so confusing about them that everyone keeps tiptoeing around the answer?

"I don't know what that means," I say. I mean, I know what *influential* means. I just don't know what it means when the word is said in that tone of voice.

"There'll be plenty of time to hear all about them," she says, and her eyes get cloudy again. "Later."

I know I've gotten all the answers I'm going to get from her today. And honestly, I'm tired of guessing. I'm tired from everything today. All I want to do is eat a hamburger the size of my face and crawl into bed with a sketchpad. I can't think of any-thing that would make me feel better than that.

* * *

Dinner wasn't hamburgers—it was chicken potpie, but that was enough to get Dad and Mya talking about pies again. When they laughed, Mom laughed, and when Mom laughed, I laughed, and it was all okay for a little while. But now that it's time for me to go to bed and do exactly what I planned to do—sketchpad and all—I can't think of anything I want to draw. Not a good sign. Obviously, my mind is elsewhere.

Because this home still doesn't feel like ours. Not in the way that it doesn't feel like ours *yet*, but in the way that it feels like it still belongs to someone else. Every time I go wandering the halls, it's hard not to feel like a burglar. I keep thinking someone is going to call the police when they see my shadow moving across the window from outside. And it wouldn't be that out of the question that someone would be watching. It feels like that's all anyone has been doing since we moved here.

When I get to the foot of the stairs, I think about the last place I felt any sort of artistic inspiration, and I remember the fake windows I painted to cover the walls in the basement. The thought of being tucked away safely down there, away from all the questions of this house and who used to live in it, comforts me enough to overcome the typical basement-at-night fear. Truly, I don't think there's ever been a person in the history of ever who didn't at least flinch at the idea of the dark spaces beneath a house.

I descend the steps to the little pad of concrete I've made my own, and there are my papers and pencils scattered just where I left them. It's weird, but drawing is the only thing I never have to chase Mya away from. It's like there's this unspoken understanding that she won't go near those. The art stuff is sacred.

The minute I pick it up, the pencil starts to move. I don't even have a picture in mind; I'm just holding the yellow, then the green, then the blue and the black. I'm letting my arm move my hand, and when I'm done, I'll see what it is that's keeping me awake.

It's an island.

But I'm probably the only one who would be able to call it that. It's not like it's obvious or anything. There's the yellow sand that drifts back and forth from the edges of the page, kind of like it's trying to decide whether or not it even wants to be on land. There's the blue water that takes up most of the paper, which is weird because I've never been big on water; I'm not the best swimmer. There's the green of the thickets of trees growing on the rocky land with its sandy beach. And there's the black.

That part's underneath.

I really don't know what to make of the black. It's not quite a geometrical design, because it's not just right angles and it's not just curved lines. I'd say it's a maze, but I think that would have to imply some sort of plan.

To me, it just looks like confusion. Lots of it. And there's so much of it, it takes up most of the space in the water.

It feels so good to finally get out of my head whatever was crowding it. I whip out another sheet from my oversized sketch-pad and set the lead to the paper, when all of a sudden, a whistling sound wafts up to my ear.

It's so faint, I can't tell if it's wind whistling or a person. Dad sometimes whistles, but I'm pretty sure he's asleep like I should be. I consider that it might just be the wind outside. Old houses make strange noises, or so Mom has said at least ten times since we've moved into Grandma and Grandpa's old house, with all its groaning floorboards and rattling pipes. Strange, though, because I don't remember it being windy at all tonight. In fact, it was super hot this afternoon.

Just when I think the sound has faded and maybe I imagined it, it starts up again, and this time, a distant but loud bang follows.

I'm on my feet before I think about it, the black pencil and sheets of paper still in my hand. This time, I could hear that it was coming from somewhere behind the wall on the other side of the basement room. The only door in here is the one leading back to the stairs, and the sound didn't come from the windows I painted onto the wood.

I hold so still, I even stop breathing for a minute. I wait for the sound to return, but the silence is even more unnerving than the whistling and the banging.

Without even scooping up the rest of my pencils, I head toward the staircase and take the first couple of steps backward, eyeing the room for what may follow me. Then, at a sprint, I thunder back up the stairs, pushing through the basement door with a little too much force, and the back of the door hits the doorstop, wobbling it on its spring.

I wince at the racket.

"Who's there?"

Every muscle in my body seizes.

"Aaron, is that you?"

The blood returns to my limbs. It's just Dad.

Walking carefully for no reason at all (considering I could have just woken the dead a second ago), I make my way down the hall to Dad's study, where I see a yellow arc of light pouring onto the dark floor. Dad's sitting figure casts a looming shadow into the lamplight.

"What're you doing up?" he asks me, not angry, but maybe a little worried. No . . . distracted.

I shrug.

Dad holds his eyes on me. "What's that in your hands?"

I look down, forgetting what I was clutching. "Just some drawings."

Dad extends his hand. He wants to see. He always wants to see.

I show him the top one first, the pirate ship I tried to draw before I lost inspiration. Dad examines the sketch closely, looking for all the details. Then, without saying a word—without even looking up—he reaches for the other picture I haven't shown him yet. Somehow, he knows this other drawing is the important one, the one I couldn't get to sleep before drawing.

When I hand it to him, he doesn't even pull it toward him. He examines it at arm's length, his eyes moving over it like he's reading text. He's so motionless, I wonder for a second if he's still with me, or if he's gone into some sort of paralysis.

His expression scares me. Not a lot, but enough to make me want to back up. I don't, though. I don't want to hurt his feelings.

When he does finally look up at me, it's like he wants me to tell him something. He wants me to guess what he's thinking.

"You don't like it," I say.

His bushy eyebrows knit together. "Why would you say that?"

I shrug.

He looks back down at the drawing, taking in the blue waters, the black veins crawling through it.

"Aaron," he says, his voice unnaturally quiet. Dad was born with a boom: Everything from his shoulders to his voice to his mustache is big. It's weird when he's quiet. "You . . . you have a . . ."

There are so many things he seems to want to say, and I don't get the impression that they're good, necessarily. Just like I don't want to offend him by backing away, he doesn't want to hurt me by telling me whatever it is I have—whatever it is he's seeing in me.

"You have a certain eye," he says, and I have no idea what he means.

"Like, artistically, or . . . ?"

He doesn't agree, but he doesn't disagree, either. Instead, he looks up at me, and I'm a little startled by it. But I'm glad he's finally looking at me. "You're capable of wondrous things," he says, and whether it's awe or fear or something in between, I can't say, but whatever it is Dad's trying to tell me, it's important.

I break eye contact long enough to look at his desk. It's only just occurred to me that Dad is awake right now, too. We're both creeping around the house in the middle of the night like robbers.

He sees me staring at his desk, at the distinct blue grids with their edges curled over the back of his desk. I haven't seen him working on blueprints since Germany. My stomach drops.

"What's that?"

Without looking down or breaking contact with me for even a second, Dad smoothly pulls a manila folder over his work and lets the outer edges of his eyes crinkle with a sad smile.

"Not a thing," he says.

I want to believe him. There was a time when I would have. There was also a time when he didn't have that sad edge to his

smiles, when he used to look at me with unconditional happiness. Now when he looks at me, it's like he's searching for answers.

Tonight, I decide to call him on it.

"Are you still proud of me?"

The crinkles around his eyes deepen.

"Of course I am," he says softly. "Why would you ask that?"

I shrug. Shrugging seems to be my thing tonight. It's so much easier than trying to come up with words.

Then Dad does something that surprises me. He takes his hands away from whatever he's covering on his desk and cups my face, making sure to hold my gaze for a good few seconds before talking.

Then he says, "Aaron, always remember this: You are incredible, and your mind is capable of incredible things."

He lets his words linger in the stagnant air of his study for a moment before asking me, "Do you understand what I mean?"

I nod as the pit in my stomach deepens.

When I walk out of his study, I'm still holding my sketches of things I don't understand and the pencil that drew them. I look at the wall above the light switch in Dad's study on my way out, eyeing the picture of my grandparents, their serious expressions and their minds that were probably capable of incredible things, too.

In bed, still wide awake, I stare at the ceiling and wonder if Dad had meant to make me feel better by saying what he said. It's so hard to tell anymore. But whatever his intentions were, what he said made me feel anything but okay.

Dad's mind is capable of incredible things, too. And look where that's gotten us.

CHAPTER 3

My mom's weird for a handful of reasons, but one of the biggies is because she likes to go grocery shopping.

"It's the best way to know you're home," she said earlier today while trying to convince Mya and me to go with her. I guess it's easier than saying she knows this wasn't supposed to be home, but things don't always work out the way we expect them to.

I suspect she really wants us to join her because she needs help carrying the bags home; Dad has the car today. And besides, Mom gets lonely.

"I have one condition," I say, and she eyes me with suspicion (as in, suspicion that she's going to cave no matter what I say, as she typically does).

"I'm listening," she says, then purses her lips.

"Strawberries," I say.

"Oh, Aaron, no," she says. "They're so expensive, and you never finish them."

"It's my only demand," I say, making myself sound very reasonable.

Mya shakes her head. "You're strange," she says.

"What? I like fruit!"

Mom sighs. "Fine, one basket. And if they don't have them, I don't want you pouting all the way home."

"Deal," I say, shaking her hand.

Mom's hands are always cold. She says it has to do with her circulation, but the rest of her is always cold, too. When she used to dance, things were different. She didn't lose her breath when she walked up the stairs. She didn't wear long cardigans everywhere and pull them closed around her. She's always been thin, but she didn't used to look this fragile. She was okay in Germany . . . we were all okay for a while. Until we weren't.

"Mya, grab the canvas bags out of the pantry, would you?"

Mya pulls a bundle of four or five bags from the closet in the kitchen, which strikes me immediately as an excellent hide-and-seek hiding place. This old house is full of those spots.

We leave through the side door in the kitchen, not even bothering to lock it. Raven Brooks is one of those towns I didn't think existed except in old movies where kids like me had paper routes and played wholesome games like hopscotch and cul-de-sac baseball.

Except I don't know if that's why Mom doesn't bother to lock our door. A part of me doubts that the rest of Raven Brooks feels so safe. It's just the way certain people act, like they're jumpy, waiting for the other shoe to drop.

Maybe Raven Brooks isn't carefree and old-fashioned. Maybe we're the ones who belong in another place and time.

* * *

The natural grocer isn't exactly *natural* as far as I can tell. More like it plays at being natural. It has these corny wooden signs that are meant to look like they're hand-painted, lemonade stand–style. Displays at the ends of aisles are propped up on shipping crates or fanned out in a halved wooden barrel. But the store itself is about a third of the size of a regular supermarket, and the bargain-brand food isn't even the generic stuff I recognize. It's cheaper imitation crackers and cookies and cereals. The meat counter is dimly lit and staffed by a single, grizzled old dude, and the produce section is little more than a corner of bins holding bananas in various stages of ripeness, small avocadoes, apples, oranges, onions, some carrots, and heads of lettuce wrapped in damp plastic.

"It's quaint!" Mom says before we can say anything.

"No strawberries," I say, pouting.

"Aaron," she scolds, "I told you we might not find them."

But I can tell by the way she's surveying the rest of the store that we're about to find out what else is hard to come by in this place.

"Let's go somewhere else," Mya says, and Mom shushes her. Mya's never really gotten the hang of the whole "indoor voice" thing.

"There isn't a 'somewhere else,'" says Mom. "Raven Brooks is an independent store–only municipality."

Mya and I look at each other.

"No chains," Mom says for clarification.

"So, you mean, like, no—" Mya starts.

Mom counts off on her fingers: "Fast food, chain supermarkets, big-box, or warehouse stores."

"You sound like a Raven Brooks brochure," I say.

"That's where I got it," she says, grimacing.

Okay, so Mom isn't a fan of this new town, either. Strangely, that makes me feel a bit better.

"Look, we're here, we need to make the best of it, and if all of us shopping at the same little town grocer is a way for us to meet our new neighbors, we might as well dive in," she says, and Mom's hard to argue with when she's being reasonable.

I hate it when she's reasonable.

Suddenly, the squeal of audio feedback fills the stuffy air of the natural grocer.

"Good morning, lovely shoppers of Raven Brooks!"

I'm trying. I really am trying. But that voice just isn't one you can help but cringe at.

We all look for the source of it, and I follow the other townspeople's gazes to the front of the store near the registers. Standing on one of the wooden crates that are used in the displays is a woman with frizzy hair and dangly, beaded earrings. I can see her frosted eyeshadow from way back here. She looks like a cross between a hippie and a roadie for one of those cheesy rock bands where the guys wear sweatbands across their foreheads.

"We have a special today on grape soda and goat cheese, made fresh by Raven Brooks's very own Nicholas Wilbanks and his lovely goats."

"Oh, I've gotta meet that guy," I whisper to Mya, who snorts. Mom puts her hand on my shoulder and squeezes hard.

"Now, the grape soda is limited to two per person," she says, and I'm not sure this lady understands the purpose of having a microphone because my ears are about to bleed. She doesn't need to yell.

"I see you trying to sneak more into your basket, Myron!" she says, waggling her finger at some guy in the middle aisle, and I think maybe the lady was expecting a laugh or two because she pauses. Crickets.

The grumpy-looking guy behind the meat counter clears his throat loudly.

The woman with the microphone wrinkles her nose, but the butcher coughs even louder, so she says, "And there's a sale on beef, too."

Then she puts the microphone down before turning off the sound system, and feedback rips through the store. I think my eardrums just exploded.

"I guess she doesn't like beef," Mya shouts at me, her hands cupped over her ears, and I hear a few people chuckle around me.

A mom with twin babies rolls by with her double-wide stroller, maneuvering it remarkably well around the narrow spaces. "Don't ask her about farm fishing," the lady says, one of her babies cooing at the toy dangling from the stroller. "Worst thirty minutes of my life."

And with that warning, she moves on, dumping cans of baby formula into the basket hooked around her arm.

Mom nods. "Well, I suppose we'd better tackle our list."

Just then, the hippie/roadie floats straight up to Mom, sidling beside her like they've known each other forever. She's what my

Grocery List

Milk

Eggs

Hamburger Buns

Waffles

Mushrooms

Strawberries

dad calls a "close talker." My mom is doing that thing where she tries to lean back but doesn't want to be rude, so instead she looks like a turtle, pushing her face back on her neck.

"We're all just so glad you and your family have joined the Raven Brooks community," the woman says.

"I—um . . . thank you?" Mom says. "Sorry, have we met?"

I start to laugh, and Mya has to yank me down the nearest aisle so I don't embarrass Mom even more. For a person who's used to performing onstage, Mom is shy one-on-one. She doesn't mean to be aloof, she's just not good at pretending.

I poke my head out of the aisle, fighting Mya off so I can watch the grocery store lady's face slip into a frown before she seems to catch herself, then laughs the fakest laugh I've ever heard.

"Oh man, this is too good. Seriously, Mouse, you're missing a show."

Mya crouches and pops her head out so we can see Mom in action.

"I should have introduced myself sooner," the woman says, but it's obvious she feels like Mom should already know who she is. "I'm but a humble proprietor in our lovely town," she says, pressing her hand over her heart. Then she gestures dramatically around the store. "The natural grocer is mine, but really, it's all of ours, you know?"

"Uh-huh," says Mom, looking around for Mya and me. We dive behind the shelf until Mom turns again to face the woman.

She sticks out her hand and makes herself smile. "I'm Diane," she says. "We just moved—"

"From Germany!" the woman interrupts, apparently knowing all of our business. My stomach tightens at the mention of our last home.

"How exotic!" she says, and Mom tilts her head at the woman. "Sorry, I still didn't catch your name."

"Marcia Tillman, at your service," the woman says, but unless her service is gossip, I'm not sure we'll have much need for her. I can almost see Mom calculating the miles to the next town over to see if we could do our grocery shopping there from now on.

"What're we hiding from?" says a voice close to my ear, and I jump, rattling the shelf of canned meats next to me.

I turn to find Enzo and Maritza holding baskets and standing beside a man in a black-and-white newsprint ballcap.

"Uh-oh," says the man in the hat. I notice the writing on the side: *Raven Brooks Banner*. "Marcia's cornered someone new," he then walks past us toward the beverage aisle. "Ooh, special on grape soda."

Maritza looks at Mya. "That's my dad. He's weird."

Mya nods. "So's mine."

Enzo has his hands on his knees, crouching like me. "So, spying's your thing, huh?"

Is it? Do I even have a "thing"? I'd never really thought about it before.

"The Petersons, back in Raven Brooks," says Mrs. Tillman. "Who would have thought?"

Up to this point, Mrs. Tillman has been nauseatingly transparent. That last remark, though . . . there's a searching look she's giving my mom, almost like she's hungry, but my mom won't feed her.

"I take it you knew my in-laws, then?" my mom says, and whatever Mrs. Tillman wanted from Mom, that wasn't it. She pinches her lips tight, her eyes moving up and down my mom before answering.

"I can't say I had the pleasure personally," says Mrs. Tillman, "but they left quite an . . . *impression* in town."

Enzo whispers, "Don't worry. She thinks she knows everybody's business, but mostly people just run the other way when they see her. Or lie."

My mom stares at Mrs. Tillman so hard, I'm surprised the grocery store lady hasn't turned to stone yet. Seems like she's made of stronger stuff than I thought. Or maybe my mom is just too nice.

"I understand your husband has quite an exciting job with the Golden Apple Corporation," says Mrs. Tillman, her voice getting a little louder, and the few people passing by are now beginning to take interest in their conversation, which obviously doesn't make my mom happy.

"Wait, what about your dad and the Golden Apple Corporation?"

The problem is, now I'm interested, too. As much as I want this obnoxious grocery woman to leave Mom alone, she's asking all the questions I haven't known how to ask since we moved to this bonkers town, and as much as I want to dive in and rescue her, I think maybe I'm about to get some answers for once.

So, like a very bad son, I lean closer to hear.

"Yes, well, I don't believe it's been officially announced yet," Mom says, sounding less in control now.

Mrs. Tillman laughs. "Oh, Diane," she says with icky familiarity, "you'll learn that Raven Brooks is positively terrible about keeping secrets. I, for one, think it's brilliant that the son of Roger and Adelle Peterson—a famed designer of amusement parks—is designing one for our very own little hometown confection."

Mrs. Tillman giggles, and it's so creepy coming out of a woman who is neither young nor innocent in any way.

Mom matches her smile. "I'm sure it's his pleasure," she says.

This is where I stop listening. It's not for lack of trying, but my heart is pumping blood so hard through my ears, it's all I can do to hear Mya, and she's standing right next to me.

"Did that lady say—?"

"Yes," I say.

"But he—"

"I know," I say.

I can't turn to face her. I know how scared she is. I can't let her see how scared *I* am.

I think we both forgot Enzo was standing there with Maritza, too, which makes it all that much worse.

"Hey, come over to my house sometime. I just got *Creeper Dawn IV.*"

If Enzo thinks he can distract me with video games . . . he's sort of right because I've forgotten all about strawberries. It'll be a little harder to distract me from what I just heard Mrs. Tillman say to Mom. And what Enzo heard, too.

It's time for me to throw Mom a lifeline.

"Is this what you were looking for?" I say, plucking the first thing I can reach off of a shelf and showing it to my mom. It's canned oysters.

She looks at me like I've just given her the last donut in the box.

"Yes!" she says, taking the oysters and dropping them in her basket. "Thank you so much, Aaron."

Enzo and Maritza take this opportunity to make their exit. I look straight at this Mrs. Tillman lady. She looks back at me with that same hungry stare she gave my mom, then moves on to Mya. It's like she wants to devour all our secrets.

"Nice store," I say to her, and she squints her eyes. "I like the buckets."

"They're authentic, aged oak barrels, actually," she says.

"Oh."

"They're *authentic*," she says again, because clearly I missed the part where I was supposed to be impressed.

70

"I have to go to the bathroom," says Mya. Sometimes the most straightforward lie is the best one.

Mom looks at Mrs. Tillman. "Well, when nature calls," she says, shrugging.

"Such a pleasure meeting you, Diane," Mrs. Tillman says way louder than she needs to, and at least five heads turn to see who the Very Important Mrs. Tillman has been talking to.

Then I start to hear the whispers.

I grab Mya's hand because I can see out of the corner of my eye that she's shaking.

"We're leaving," Mom murmurs to me, dodging the stares as we head for the door. She ditches the basket with the oysters on one of the *authentic* wooden barrels before throwing the door wide and making a break for it. We have to struggle to keep pace with her on the way home.

"Mom?" Mya tries, but Mom isn't having any of it, not right now.

"We'll order pizza tonight," she says, but she knows that's not what we want to talk to her about.

So instead of cheering for pizza, we take longer strides so we don't fall behind on the way home.

* * *

Raven Brooks's only grocery store may not be anything to get excited about, but Raven Brooks's only pizza parlor is a different story. I'm ready to fight Mya to the death for the last slice of mushroom and black olive.

71

"If you value your life, back away," Mya says, staring me down.

"How can you eat as much as you eat? Like, how is it humanly possible?"

"I'm capable of extraordinary feats," says Mya, and frankly, I don't doubt it.

"Excuse me, but I think our guest is entitled to the last slice," Mom says, motioning to Mr. Gershowitz.

I don't quite know why, but I never pictured my dad with a friend. Like, ever. He just doesn't seem like the "friend" type. Not like that's a bad thing. He just always seems to be so busy working or thinking about work, it never occurred to me that he'd have an old buddy from school. Especially not one like Mr. Gershowitz.

He's nothing like my dad. He's probably the most easygoing person I've ever met in my life. He has this way of looking like he's leaning back even when he's not, like he can't make his body get worked up about anything. He laughs a lot, but not in an annoying way. Just a quiet chuckle. I can see why Dad's friends with him.

"It's okay, Diane. I'll bust if I have one bite more," he says.

"Liar," Dad says congenially. "You could pack away an entire pie if you wanted to."

"Don't have the metabolism I used to have," says Mr. Gershowitz, shaking his head. "Not all of us are built like football players."

"You played football?" Mya asks.

Both Dad and Mr. Gershowitz laugh at that. "He didn't make

it past the first round of tryouts," says Dad's friend. I wait for Dad to take offense to that, but he just shakes his head. It's almost like Mr. Gershowitz's calm is contagious. I think this is the most relaxed dinner we've had since we moved here.

"I had different ambitions anyway," Dad says, and he and Mr. Gershowitz get all dreamy-eyed.

"You wouldn't believe the trouble your dad and I could get into when we were younger."

"Oh, I need to hear this," I say. The only thing weirder than imagining Dad with a friend is imagining Dad getting into trouble.

Well, *normal* trouble. Kid trouble. Not Germany trouble.

Suddenly, the pizza isn't sitting too well.

"Ike's exaggerating," Dad says.

"That's a fine way of dodging your delinquent past," Mr. Gershowitz says, and things are starting to rumble below. "We used to make so much trouble at your parents' office, they'd send us out into the forest with all the poison ivy just to keep us from getting underfoot!"

Suddenly, something in the room shifts.

Mom's eyes grow as big as quarters, and Dad's face turns to stone. It seems like the only person who hasn't caught onto the sudden change is Mr. Gershowitz.

"But I thought you said Grandma and Grandpa worked from home," I say to Dad, and that only seems to make things worse.

"I think it's time to call it a night," says Dad. "Ike has to get to work anyway."

Then he turns to his friend, his face completely unreadable.

Except this time, it seems to be Mr. Gershowitz who understands, even though the rest of us don't.

"I suppose you're right," he says to my dad, matching his stoniness.

"Oh no, so soon?" says Mom, but I can tell she isn't really trying to get him to stay. What the heck is going on here?

Three chairs scrape the floors as the grown-ups stand stiffly, leaving Mya and me at the table with the last slice.

"Mine," says Mya, recovering quickly from the awkwardness.

I don't fight her. My appetite has officially died. Between memories of Germany, this morning's encounter at the grocery store, and whatever just happened, it's a wonder my stomach hasn't turned itself fully inside out by now.

I look at Mya and wonder how she's doing it. But I know better. She's taking it all in, too. She just has different ways of dealing. Her torment comes at night.

I hear the front door close a little harder than it needs to, and my parents mutter something that gets loud for a second before dying back down. All I catch was "don't understand" and "worry yourself" before I hear Dad retreat to his study down the back hallway.

When Mom returns, she smooths her hands over her skirt and pretends nothing happened.

"We'll have to order from this pizza place again!" she says, her voice that weird, high-pitched chirp she gets when she's covering something up.

"Pretty sure we don't have a choice," I say.

"Good point."

* * *

I can't sleep that night. It was lights out almost two hours ago, but I can't get my stomach to settle. At first I tell myself it's just the pizza, but I'm an even worse liar when I'm trying to lie to myself. The day's conversations are circling my brain like a flushed toilet, and after another fifteen minutes of tossing and turning, I head downstairs for a glass of water.

I don't even make it to the kitchen before I see the glow of light coming from Dad's study, which is weird because I could have sworn I heard him go to bed over an hour ago.

It's impossible to do much actual creeping in this house, with every floorboard making a different sound when you step on it, but I move as quietly as I can down the little back hall.

When I get to the door, it's cracked just enough for me to see not my dad, but my mom, sitting at the desk piled high with papers scrawled with notes and designs. Her head is in her hands, and though she isn't moving, I can hear her sniffling softly.

I don't mean for her to notice me there, but the stupid floors . . .

"Oh! Aaron, I didn't hear you," Mom says, wiping her face like it's the most natural thing in the world for her to be sitting alone in Dad's study crying at night.

No kid should ever see their parents cry. No matter how old I am, it feels like something at the core of the earth is rupturing when I see my mom cry. It doesn't happen often, but when it does, the only thing I want to do is dig a hole and bury myself.

Anyway, we're both here instead of sleeping, and we're both

thinking about something that needs to be shared, even if it's just with each other.

"What that lady at the grocery store said today . . ." I begin, *and please fill in the rest.* I'm begging her to please say the rest.

"Go on back to sleep, Cat."

Cat. She hasn't called me Cat in over a year. I remember the last time. It was four in the morning in Germany, and I'd caught her in a moment just like this, when we both should have been sleeping, but neither of us were. It was when things were starting to get bad, and at the time, it brought me so much comfort to hear her call me that name like she used to. Her two kids, Cat and Mouse.

It doesn't have the same effect anymore, which makes me feel even worse.

"I can't," I tell her, then stare at the pile of papers her elbows are resting on. She carefully moves some folders over the tops of the most exposed papers without breaking eye contact with me. It's an eerily familiar move.

"What do we do when we can't sleep?" she asks me. Because we all have a method in this household. At some point or another, all four of us are plagued by fits of sleeplessness. It's a family legacy.

"Think of the bright places," I say, less from belief and more from rote memory. I think about the fake windows I hung in the basement, painted with sunshiny days, the vibrant pictures I've plastered my bedroom walls with, all their yellows and minty greens and light blues.

I'm trying, Mom. But the darkness always seems to find us.

"I know you're worried," Mom says in a rare moment of candidness. "But this place is going to be different, Cat. This place is going to be a new beginning for us."

She's so close to being convincing. If I were to close my eyes, I bet I could almost fool myself into believing her, that Raven Brooks really will be different, and that we can simply erase everything we left behind—everything we escaped halfway around the world.

But I can see her eyes, even with the meager light my dad's desk lamp puts out. The edges of her eyelids are rimmed in pink, and why else would she be crying unless she weren't just as convinced as I am that things are already starting to fall apart?

I give her one more chance to tell me what she's really thinking.

"So, you think moving here was the right thing to do?"

Mom stares at me in the doorway for what feels like a very long time before saying, "I wouldn't have done it any other way."

I tell her good night and go back to my room with her words chasing one another through my head.

I wouldn't have done it any other way.

Which isn't the right thing to do. It's more like the *only* thing we could do.

It's some time before I finally hear my mom pad up the stairs and slip back into her room where Dad is sleeping. I wait even longer to make sure she won't be awake to hear me go back downstairs.

The door to Dad's study is closed, but it's not locked. The folders Mom slid over the papers are still there. When I reach for the folders to scoot them over, I have to work to steady my shaking hand.

Think of the bright places, I tell myself. But it's far too dark in this room for that.

I see that the first paper is a photocopy of a contract carrying my dad's signature, along with a scribbled signature from someone at the Golden Apple Corporation.

I take a full breath in and push it out. So, it's official. My dad will design a new amusement park for the Golden Apple Corporation, whatever that is.

That would have been enough truth to swallow for one night, but the light blue schematic rolled at the top and bottom edges underneath the signature page is impossible to ignore, so I move the contract aside.

What I see is the worst kind of omen.

There, sketched and erased and sketched over, with recalculated steepness and near impossible angles, is the beginnings of a roller coaster that makes terror its priority. I've seen a schematic like this, only instead of rails and ties and golden apples, the previous one had water and boats. But those same steep drops, those same inhuman climbs—they all looked just like this.

He wouldn't risk making the same mistake again.

I so badly want this to be true. I'm willing to do almost anything I can to believe it.

But the truth is written all over his desk.

THEODORE MASTERS PETERSON

MARVIN STEVENSON

CHAPTER 4

Enzo has an actual game room, a space that's bigger than my bedroom, with no door or closet, so it's more like a loft on the second story of their house. It's one of those places my mom would call a "rumpus room," which always sounded ridiculously old-fashioned to me.

Anyway, "game room" is the perfect name for it, because Enzo has basically every video game ever made, and Mya and Maritza are quickly making their way through that entire collection.

"How do I punch?" Mya says frantically, jamming her thumbs against the buttons.

"Well not like *that*," says Maritza. "You look like you're trying to dance."

Mya's character flails and dips while a three-headed beast lunges through the air.

"Not even rhythm can save you now!" I taunt her from the other end of the room. Enzo and I had to choose: We could either let our sisters have a turn, or Enzo's dad was going to make us watch a documentary on water fowl.

No one said we couldn't give them a hard time, though.

"Go back to your lame book project," Maritza says to me with the same level of comfort she tells her own brother to bug off, and I can't help but feel flattered.

Enzo pulls me back into our discussion, which isn't about a book project, even though Enzo sort of wants it to be.

"Dude, I'm telling you, we could make a comic book series or something," he says, watching my hand closely.

It started as a butterfly, but my drawing took a dark turn—that happens sometimes—and now I've created a sort of mutant moth-man, with a twisted body and frayed wings, and he's standing in the wreckage of a town he's just destroyed.

"I dunno," I say, adding some shading to the side of the moth guy's face. "It's just sort of something I do for fun."

That's not true. Half the time I draw without even realizing what my hand is doing. All I know for sure is that it feels better when my hand is moving, and when I finish a drawing, I'm always a little sad. Which I guess is why I keep doing it, so I never have to finish.

"Or like a comic strip, for the school paper!" he says, either not hearing or not caring about my lack of enthusiasm.

"Why don't you talk to your dad?" I say. "You like to write; your dad works at the newspaper. I bet he could hook you up with some sort of . . . I don't know, internship or something?"

"Nah, Dad isn't like that," Enzo says, the excitement draining from his voice. "Dad's all about making it on your own merits, no special favors. Besides, he wants me to be an accountant or a nurse or something."

Enzo turns his notebook to a blank page, hiding the words he showed me earlier, which were actually really good.

"Don't get me wrong," says Enzo. "He's super into what he does, but he doesn't want me or my sister doing it. He says it's not stable enough, whatever that means."

Enzo looks embarrassed, like I might think differently of him now because maybe they haven't always been the type of family to have a game room or a house in New Town. The thing is, though, I know exactly what his dad means by *unstable*.

"My mom is sort of the same," I say, because I've seen the way she fidgets and distracts herself when she sees me drawing. It's not that she isn't proud of me; I think she just sees me looking like Dad.

Enzo's quiet, and after a second, I realize it might be because I mentioned my mom, and his own mom died when he was really young. I didn't get the impression that it was an off-limits subject, necessarily. I mean, *he* was the one who told *me* after I basically wouldn't stop staring at the mountain of framed pictures on their mantel. But now Enzo is staring at the middle of the table we're standing around, his notebook in front of him, my sketchpad in front of me, and I wonder if maybe I've said too much.

It's something else he's thinking about, though.

"Hey, don't tell anyone I said that. About my dad, I mean," he says. "Okay?"

I nod right away, a little surprised. "I won't."

"Thanks."

It's that easy. He gave me a secret and asked me to hang on to it, and all of a sudden, I'm trusted. For the first time in a long time, I'm holding on to a secret that isn't mine or my weird family's.

It feels pretty great.

"And *that's* how you behead a Gorgon," says Maritza from across the room, setting her controller down triumphantly.

"If I ever make it to the center of the earth, I'm taking you with me," says Mya, in awe of her new friend.

"Okay, but I have piano lessons on Wednesdays," says Maritza, completely serious.

"My dad's making carnitas tonight," says Enzo.

"I'll go tell him you guys are eating over," Maritza says, springing to her feet without asking if we want to.

We do, though.

* * *

If my dad were the friend-making type, I bet he'd be friends with Mr. Esposito. Maybe I expected him to be sad because his wife had died a long time ago or stressed because his job at the newspaper was hard, but it turns out Enzo and Maritza's dad is really cool. He's intense, but almost like he's on the other side of intense from where my dad is.

"But then a squirrel chewed through the camera cables, and we were able to get the story out first," he says, putting a big pile of shredded pork on a plate next to some potatoes and handing it to Mya.

He's telling us how the *Raven Brooks Banner* scooped the cocky reporters from the TV station—"forfeit by rodent," he'd called it—but it doesn't really matter what he's talking about because he can make anything a story.

"If there's a rodent involved, Dad has a story about it," Maritza says, pulling Mya into the seat next to her.

"You have had a weird number of vermin encounters," says Enzo.

"Did I ever tell you about the rat poop incident from college? My roommate had this hazmat suit, and—"

"Maybe rat poop can wait until after dinner?" Maritza says, her fork just below her mouth.

"Ah, of course," says Mr. Esposito, then stares wistfully into his memory. "Good 'ole Jay. I wonder what ever happened to him. I should look him up."

I tell Mr. Esposito that I've never had carnitas this good before, which is the truth, and he manages to accept the compliment graciously and quickly dismiss it all at the same time.

Instead, he turns the topic to Mya and me.

"So, we're in the presence of a couple of local celebrities," he says, and I hope he isn't going where I think he's going with this.

I glance at Enzo, who looks a little sheepish, but he doesn't know it's a much more touchy subject than it should be. "I may have told him about your grandparents."

So much for my appetite.

"I bet your dad's parents told you some pretty fantastic stories from their heyday here in Raven Brooks," says Mr. Esposito, not slowing his eating even a little. He's digging, though. I guess that's what you do when you work at a newspaper.

It suddenly occurs to me why Enzo might have invited me over. I'd be lying if I said it didn't sting a little.

"Actually, we never met them," I say to Mr. Esposito, hopeful that this might cut the conversation short.

Then Mr. Esposito does something surprising—he comes clean.

"Sorry," he says to Mya and me. "I promised the kids I wouldn't bring it up. They didn't want to embarrass you," he says.

I look again at Enzo, and I feel at least a little better about him.

"I'm nosy," says Mr. Esposito, not at all ashamed. "The town owes a lot to your grandparents and the work they did when they were alive."

Because he's being so honest, I decide to take a chance, too. "What . . . what was their work?"

Mr. Esposito's face falls. "Well, that's the thing. I was hoping you and your sister would be able to shed a little light on that.

85

Your grandparents were . . . do you know what *mercurial* means?"

I nod, even though, not really, no.

"They were always something of a mystery," says Mr. Esposito, sensing my bluff. "I suppose all geniuses are."

I immediately think of my dad, and this is where my stupid, slow brain finally makes the connection.

My grandparents had secrets to keep, just like my dad docs. Just like my whole family does, apparently. Some people get inheritances. We get a weird old house and a billion questions.

"My parents don't really talk about them," Mya says, looking ashamed. I don't want her to look that way. She didn't do anything to deserve that.

Mr. Esposito smiles kindly, even though I can tell he's disappointed that we're as clueless as he is.

"Talking about people who are gone can be painful for some," he says, and I don't mean to, but I look over my shoulder at the mantel in their family room, the piles of framed photos of his late wife glittering under the overhead light.

When I turn back around, I see him catch me staring, and instead of clamming up, he says, "She was a wonder."

So, this is what it feels like to live out in the open, no secrets to protect, no topics to tiptoe around.

* * *

At home that night, I lie in bed asking myself why Mr. Esposito said all those things about my dad's parents. He was probably just being nice. That would be the normal, nonparanoid response to somebody being polite. But I'm not normal, and paranoia is quickly becoming my next best skill after lockpicking.

I think back to everyone who's had anything to say about my grandparents in the short time we've lived in Raven Brooks: Mr. Esposito, Mr. Gershowitz, Mr. Donaldson, even that grocery store lady, Mrs. Tillman. They'd all told me how important my grandparents' work was. So why did it always sound like they were about to say something else?

In fact, the only person who's said anything different is that jerk from eighth period. What had he called them? The *town wingnuts*?

Maybe all those people who said nice things were just trying to cushion a blow. Tell me all the good things about them before I hear what they really mean to say . . . that they were "mercurial." Troubled. Maybe even dangerous.

From the other room, I hear Mya cry out suddenly.

I can usually tell a nightmare from the sound of her voice, but I'm still getting used to all the echoes in this house, so I creep into her room quietly.

Her forehead is pinched into folds, and I can see from the glow of her pink night-light that her eyes are moving around behind her eyelids.

I kneel beside her bed and push the hair away from her face.

"It's okay, Mouse. It's not real. Not anymore," I whisper over and over again, until the lines on her forehead smooth over and the scream that's caught in her throat dies.

I pick up her little rag doll from the floor and tuck it into the crook of her elbow. Then I pull the red jewelry box down from her dresser and open it to reveal the little ballerina on its spring in front of the mirror. I tip the box over and wind the bar until the ballerina begins to turn to her little mechanical song.

Mya is silent and still.

Back in my room, I do my best to be silent and still, too. But Mya's sleeping nightmare has become my waking one, and suddenly, I'm back in Germany.

Ripples of chaos and shouts come from the flume ride at the far end of Fernweh Welt. I'm holding Mya's hand and pulling her toward the ride, but there are so many people just standing around watching that we have to weave in and out of them. They're all staring, but not us. We're looking at the ground so we don't trip. We're looking up so we can find our way. We're looking everywhere but at each other because that would only confirm our deepest fears.

Then I hear Mom's voice calling from the base of the ride, telling us to come quick, and then there's no denying something horrible has happened because her face is so pale and her eyes are so wide.

"The cart didn't detach. Your father—" Mom says, her voice raspy and hoarse.

I take off running up the ramp to the line, and I hear Mya and my mom sprinting after me.

"Aaron, no! It's not safe!" I can hear my mom scream.

But I'm faster, and I have to see for myself.

"Aaron!" she keeps screaming.

I hear her voice screaming for the rest of the night, crying out my name until it blurs into one continuous wail in my ears. I drift in and out of sleep hearing that cry, until I'm mostly convinced that her screams are coming from somewhere in the house, in the form of a high, distant howl.

CHAPTER 5

I'm on Ms. Gresham's list, which is evidently scandalous. She has an actual list that she keeps in her apron pocket, and she's had it for so long, its corners are curled and the paper itself is yellowed. Some say there are kids on that list dating back as far as the 1970s.

"Oh man, you're never getting off that list. It's in stone now," Enzo says to me once we get to Civics.

"What does that even mean?"

"I don't know, but I'm staying on her good side. They say the list brings misfortune," says Enzo.

"You sound like an old-timey villager. She's not the town sorcerer," I say.

"Go ask Tony Rambino about the list," says Enzo, like I'm supposed to know who that is.

"All I did was fall asleep in her class!"

"So did Tony Rambino, and he's had nothing but bad luck ever since. I heard he got bit by a gecko once. Do you know how hard it is to get a gecko to bite you?"

"I think the bigger mystery is why she wears an apron to teach literature," I say.

This quiets Enzo for a second, and I take that second to put my head back down in Civics. I'm not going to make it until the end of the day.

The bell rings, and Mr. Donaldson calls the class to attention. Enzo scoots his chair back hard enough to thump my desk, and my head slips from my arms to the hard wood.

"Dude, a concussion is the last thing I need right now," I say.

"The *last thing you need* is another teacher hating you," Enzo says, and even though half of me (maybe a little more than half) wants to punch him in the face, the other half is touched that he cares.

"Announcement time," says Mr. Donaldson, and whatever the announcement is, he sounds less than thrilled about it.

"This Friday, we'll be joining the elementary students—"

The class groans one collective, agonized protest.

"*A*hem!" Mr. Donaldson says, and the class settles. He tries again. "On Friday, we'll be joining the elementary students on a field trip—"

The class breaks into cheers, all hands slapping and feet stomping.

"ENOUGH!" Mr. Donaldson roars, and the class hushes fast. "One more word before I get this sentence out, and you'll be spending Friday sweeping out animal pens for the Future Farmers of America."

The threat of manure. Works every time.

"On Friday, we'll be joining the elementary students for a field trip to the Golden Apple factory."

Crickets. Every set of eyes searches the room for the one who might dare to crack the silence.

Mr. Donaldson sighs. "Now you may display your enthusiasm."

The class cheers, mostly. There are those who are thrilled,

like Enzo. There are those who are confused, like that kid in the corner who sucks on her eraser. And then there is me. I'm pretty sure I'm the only one not exactly looking forward to learning more about the illustrious Golden Apple Company—not now that I know they're the reason we're here. The reason why Dad is designing a new park.

Then there's Mr. Donaldson. He looks even more glum than I feel about it.

He raps his knuckles hard on his desk. "Some of you may be wondering how it is that the school board has approved a return trip to the Golden Apple factory after . . . the *incident* . . ." he says, and if he was hoping to mask the intrigue by referring to it that way, it's not working. Every kid in the class is now leaning forward, ears pricked for scandal.

I have zero idea what's going on.

"However, in their infinite wisdom, the school board has elected to give this year's students a second chance."

Okay, so Mr. Donaldson is *not* a fan of the school board. Got it.

"Books open to page ninety-seven," he says, changing direction fast enough to give me whiplash. But the rest of the class—even the eraser sucker—shifts just as fast, slapping books on desks and flipping pages.

"Well," I mumble to myself. "At least I'm not tired anymore."

* * *

As soon as the bell rings, Enzo has me by the sleeve, and we're joined in the middle of the courtyard by Maritza and Mya.

"Friday!" Maritza says excitedly to Enzo. "Think of all the free samples! Wait . . . do you think they'll have the Granny Smith Fizzies? They're not supposed to be out before Halloween, but—"

Enzo waves her off. "Yeah yeah." He turns to me, earning a death stare from Maritza.

"Do you know what this means?"

"I can honestly say I have absolutely no idea what this means," I say.

That's not exactly true. It means that I get to spend all of Friday being reminded that we traveled 4,700 miles fleeing one nightmare only to fall headlong into another. I'm starting to wonder if we're ever going to wake up.

One glance at Mya tells me she's wondering the same thing. She's chewed her nails down to the quick.

"It means Enzo has to spend an entire day with her, Aaron. An *entire day.*"

Her . . . her . . .

"Trinity," Maritza says, helping me out.

"Right. Trinity," I say.

Enzo looks hurt that I didn't remember. "Sorry, I'm just tired."

"Well, wake up, because you gotta help me make an unforgettable impression."

I stare at this skinny guy, skinnier than me, which is saying a lot: his bushy eyebrows and metal-bracketed teeth, his massive Converse sneakers that he trips over at least three times a day— because nobody could walk with feet that big, let's face it.

"I think you'd be pretty hard to forget," I tell him, and he smiles.

"Okay then, *irresistible*."

"Gross," says Maritza.

"Gross?" Enzo says, remembering his sister again. "I'm not the one who ate an entire block of Velveeta last night."

"I'm not embarrassed," Maritza says defiantly. "Badge of honor. I have an iron stomach."

"We'll see how proud you are when your farts smell like grilled cheese," he said, and Maritza turned a shade of crimson I've never actually seen.

Then Enzo turns that same shade of red, and I can't understand why until I turn to see what he can't stop staring at.

Trinity is walking beside another girl who looks a little younger than us, maybe even younger than Mya. Maritza's face lights up as her blush fades.

"Hey!" she squeezes past Enzo and me to sling her arm around the younger girl. "We have a new friend. She's super cool. She plays *Creeper Dawn*."

The girl smiles kindly at my sister, so I like her immediately.

"I'm Lucy," she says, giving Mya a little wave.

Trinity looks at Enzo.

"So, the Golden Apple factory this Friday," she says, and I can't tell if she's excited. I almost get the impression she just wants to see what Enzo will say. Or maybe she's just trying to see if she can get him to speak again.

It's not looking good.

Suddenly, the girl named Lucy reaches for my sister's arm and pulls her from our circle.

"Okay, so I'm your After-School Buddy," she tells Mya.

"My After-School—?"

"Basically, the person who takes you to see all the clubs and sports and stuff," Lucy says.

"Oh," says Mya, and I can tell she's nervous about going off with this girl she's never met, even if she seems nice.

"Lucy's the extracurricular queen. If there's a scoreboard or a membership roster, you're going to see 'Yi' on it. The girl's unstoppable," Trinity says.

"They have clubs in elementary school here?" I ask, more than a little surprised.

Lucy flashes a smile. "It's like my mom always says, *You're never too young to start building your résumé.*"

Trinity then turns to me, catching me off guard. "You're on Friday, Peterson," she says. "I'm your After-School Buddy."

My face is scorching, but it's nothing compared to Enzo's. He's looking at me like he's going to write a country song about how I betrayed him.

All I can do is shrug, or I'll blow his cover.

"You'll need to know which clubs to *avoid*," Maritza says quietly to Mya while Lucy is distracted. "I'll come with you."

I immediately see Mya relax, and I send up a silent thanks to Maritza.

The girls pull my sister away, who looks back at me with a smile, and I give her a half wave so nobody thinks I'm a dork.

I mean, they'll have plenty of time to figure that out later.

"Your sister will be fine with Lucy," Trinity reassures me. "The girl may only be seven, but she practically runs the school. Her mom's head of the PTA."

"Okay," I say, turning on my heel away from the school. "So who's gonna fill me in on the 'incident'?"

Enzo and Trinity blink at me, and I wonder for a second if last period was just a fever dream. I'm still pretty groggy from last night.

"The reason Mr. Donaldson's all bent out of shape about our field trip Friday?" I try again.

"Ah, right," says Trinity, catching on.

"So, maybe five or so years ago—"

"Six," Enzo says, finally remembering how to talk at the weirdest possible moment.

Trinity furrows her brow. "Okay . . . *six* years ago, the middle school kids were doing their Golden Apple factory field trip. It was an annual thing," she says, rolling her eyes, but I can tell she's proud of her town. Enzo told me her parents are really big into community involvement, so I guess it shouldn't surprise me that the enthusiasm trickled down to Trinity.

"Anyway," she continues, "these three kids thought it'd be a good idea to sneak away from the tour and go hang out in the woods."

I look to Enzo for clarification. "The factory is pretty deep in the woods."

"Ah. Thanks."

"When it was time to get on the buses, the chaperones noticed they were missing, and there was this huge search of the factory and the woods. People started saying things like they'd fallen into one of the factory grinders or gotten squished by the train or something," Trinity says, and I can't help but notice her eyes getting wider as she talks.

"So, what happened to them?" I say.

Enzo shakes his head slowly. "Nobody knows."

I can actually hear myself swallow. "You mean, they never found them?"

"Oh, they found them," says Enzo.

I look back at Trinity.

"It wasn't until much later that night. They were so deep in the woods, even the police couldn't believe they'd gotten that far. But that wasn't the weirdest part."

"They were so freaked, they couldn't even talk," Enzo says, his eyes as wide as Trinity's now.

"What do you mean, 'they couldn't talk'?"

"I mean they didn't say a word," Enzo says. "Not where they'd been. Not what they'd seen. *Nothing.*"

We're all quiet for a minute, and even though it's warm outside, I have to smooth the hairs down on my arms.

"I have to see the woods," I say, and both Trinity and Enzo look at me like I've suddenly sprouted antennae.

"Nope," Enzo says, understanding before Trinity this time. "Not happening."

"Oh, come on!" I say. "You can't tell me a story like that and expect me to just let it lie."

"It really is a bad idea," Trinity says, technically disagreeing with me, even though it somehow sounds more like she's agreeing with me. There's a smile hiding somewhere behind her eyes.

"It's a *terrible* idea!" Enzo says, seeming to sense that he's losing his ally. "Setting aside the fact that there's poison ivy in there," he says, pausing for dramatic effect. But when neither of us takes the bait, he keeps going, "no one maintains the forest on that side of the factory; there's only the road leading into it on the other side, and the train tracks."

"It's a forest," I say, and I'm not trying to embarrass Enzo, but come on. How scary can a bunch of trees and squirrels be?

"Well . . ." Trinity says, this time looking a little doubtful. "It's . . . uh . . . more than that. Or at least some people think so."

And by *some people*, Trinity obviously means herself. And Enzo. They trade a look I can't read, but there's something they haven't shared with me yet.

"Okay," I say, playing along. "I'm listening."

"Don't laugh," Enzo says.

"I never laugh," I say, and they both look a little perplexed, like they're trying to remember a time when I have. Good luck. Some people just aren't laughers.

"Forest Protectors," says Trinity, and nothing else. Like I'm supposed to get everything I need from "Forest Protectors."

"Yeah, I think I need you to elaborate a little."

Enzo takes a deep breath. "They protect the forest from strangers. Some say they look like a cross between a person and a crow."

"So Crow People. Is this some sort of new-kid hazing thing?"

They look at each other like they're trying to decide if it is. It surprises me that it's Trinity who says the next part.

"It used to be that they only protected the forest, mostly from kids messing around where they weren't supposed to. But over time, they developed a taste for the blood of children."

I look from Trinity to Enzo, Enzo to Trinity. I wait for one of them to bust up laughing, having lured the new kid right into their stupid story about Crow People who eat kids for kicks. But neither of them so much as cracks a smile, and I'm left with this one conclusion: They totally believe this story.

"I just have to say it; you both know you sound completely *verrückt*, right?"

They're back to giving me the antennae look again.

"Completely what now?" says Enzo.

"Is that German?" says Trinity. "My mom did a study abroad there in college! It means loony, right?"

"Something like that," I say, and I hate myself so much right now. The last—I mean *very dead last*—thing I want to do is talk about Germany.

"Anyway, the Crow People," I say.

"Forest Protectors," Trinity corrects.

"Right. So let me see if I have this right. The school board hasn't let anyone tour the Golden Apple factory for five—"

"Six," says Enzo.

"—*six* years because a few kids went missing for an afternoon, and everyone just assumes that the most natural explanation is that they were carried off by half-human-half-bird hybrids?"

Well, it worked. We aren't talking about Germany anymore.

"When you put it like that . . ." says Enzo, not liking me very much at the moment, not that I can blame him.

"Okay, let me put it a different way," I say, trying a more

diplomatic approach. "What else have we got to do this after-noon besides exploring a creepy forest?"

Enzo is hating me more by the second, judging by the way his eyes keep growing bigger. But Trinity hasn't said no yet, and if I could figure out a way to tell them that I'm desperate for any distraction from my messed-up family situation, I'd try that. But as bad as I am at lying, I'm even worse at telling the truth, so instead I suggest exploring.

"Look," says Trinity to Enzo, "we can leave a trail just in case. Then there's no way we'll get lost."

"I'm not scared," says Enzo, though literally no one said he was.

And this time I do try lying because it seems like the least I can do for Enzo after putting him in a completely unwinnable situation.

"Well, I am," I say. "So at least you're braver than me."

"C'mon, I'll protect you both," says Trinity, forging a path forward, presumably toward the woods.

Enzo gives me a look before falling in line behind her. It's somewhere between *I could kill you* and *thanks*, and I think he's leaning a little more toward *thanks*. I'm going to tell myself that anyway.

* * *

I'm surprised to find that the path that leads into the forest isn't that far from my house. I guess I shouldn't be surprised, though.

It's not like I've done all that much exploring outside of Friendly Court. I know that we live on an old street—in a house that was built before the newer development went up several blocks away, where Enzo lives. It's just a feeling, but I get the impression that people have opinions about people who live in the old part of town versus the newer neighborhoods. People get weird when they think they have more money than other people.

"It's just through there," says Enzo, pointing down a narrow alleyway behind a row of houses.

I swallow. I was lying about being afraid before, but not so much anymore. Narrow alleys aren't my first choice for hangouts.

"Here, let me," says Trinity charitably, and I don't argue.

She picks her way around the weeds growing up in the cracks between the cinder-block walls and the open field that's exposed through a break in the wall. We duck through the hole and into the field, and from there, a different kind of wall stretches before us: one made entirely of the tallest trees I've ever seen.

"Perfect home for a half-human-half-bird hybrid, huh?" says Enzo, and I'm rethinking what I believed was a silent *thanks* from before. He's definitely enjoying my fear now.

Trinity takes us to an opening, if you can call it that. It's an overgrown footpath that was at some point cleared of its brush. That's not the case anymore, though. Thorny blackberry vines and what I'm nearly positive is poison ivy crisscross the path.

"You know the old 'leaves of three' saying, right?" says Trinity.

"Yep, 'leaves of three, leave 'em be or you'll be a swollen itchy red mess for weeks and all your friends will laugh at you.' That's how it goes, right?" I say, still staring at the vines.

"Precisely," she says, and takes a tiny leap over the first tangle of growth and into the immediate darkness of the forest.

Enzo follows her, and he lands with a little yelp I'm sure he didn't mean for anyone to hear. I'm last, and I practically have to do a gymnastic tuck jump to get over the clump of death plants, and when I fall safely on the other side, I let out an even louder yelp than Enzo did.

"Nice landing," says Enzo.

We pick our way through the woods in silence to start with, training most of our attention on the plants to avoid. After a while, though, we seem to have caught a rhythm, and the path appears to have widened just enough for us to walk normally instead of tightrope-style. It feels like we've been walking for some time, but we were moving pretty slowly at first, so who knows.

"So, Forest Protectors," I say.

"We don't really have to talk about that right now, do we?" says Enzo.

"Has anyone ever actually seen one of these things?" I say.

"Depends who you ask," Trinity says. "It's always somebody who knows somebody who saw one once."

Weirdly, I'm a little disappointed. So much about this town is wacky, I was sort of hoping they'd be a little more original than dragging around an urban legend about a mysterious local creature. They get points for originality, though. Man-bird combo is one I've never heard before. And apparently there's a whole flock of them.

"Then there's the nests, of course," says Enzo, and this stops me for a second.

"Sorry, nests?"

"I don't know if you can call them nests as much as habitats," says Trinity. "I think because people have mostly found them in the trees, they just refer to them as nests."

"In the trees?"

"Yeah," Enzo says. "Pretty high up, too. It even got the university's attention. They sent some bird scientists out here, what're they called?"

"Ornithologists," says Trinity without turning.

"Right, those. Anyway, they sent bird doctors out or whatever, and they studied the nests, and none of them could figure out what would make a nest that big."

"Um . . . how about weirdos trying to scare a town into believing there are bird people in the woods?" I say, but I know I sound a little desperate because now we're talking about actual scientists who don't have answers.

"Yeah, they considered that," says Trinity. "But there was some animal rights organization that got involved at that point, and they prevented the scientists from removing the nests from where they'd been found. Without being able to study them in a lab, the ornithologists sort of dropped it."

"Dropped it?" I say. "That feels a little unscientific."

"Or people just stopped talking about it. I don't know," says Trinity, distracted. "Hey, I thought I was taking us in the direction of the factory, but—"

"But what?" I ask, feeling more on edge than when we started this little journey I insisted on.

"None of this looks familiar," she says.

"What's 'familiar'?" says Enzo. "It's just a bunch of trees. It all looks the same."

I think Enzo and I are competing for most uptight. He might be in the lead.

"Things have changed a lot since the last time I was here," says Trinity, and now even she sounds a little worried.

None of us, though, is prepared for the distant rumble of thunder that ripples through the sky.

"I'm not the only one who heard that, right?" I say.

"Nope," says Enzo.

"It's okay," says Trinity. "We don't really need to worry until we see ligh—"

A bolt of lightning illuminates the sky that's suddenly roiling with heavy gray clouds.

"We should go," she says, her tone shifting in the space of a second.

Fat drops begin to fall from above, tapping the tops of the leaves at first, but the tree canopy only protects us for a minute. Soon, the rain begins breaking through.

"Okay, we're turning around!" says Trinity, officially losing her cool.

We spin in the opposite direction, and Enzo, who was in the middle, cuts to the front of the line, giving us a running start.

The leaves are quickly growing slick, and the dirt beneath our feet is a river of mud within minutes. We move fast, no longer careful of the plants or the vines, no longer picking our way through. Instead, we crash around, dodging low-hanging branches and the buckets of rain suddenly pummeling us.

When we reach a fork in the path that I don't remember facing on the way into the woods, we all stop.

"Which way?" Trinity says, looking straight at Enzo.

"How should I know?"

"You're kidding, right?" she says, not laughing.

But neither is Enzo. "Why would I be kidding?"

"Because you're the one who was leaving the trail," she says.

"Says who?" Enzo squeaks, having to raise his voice over the thunder.

"Why would I be doing it? I was navigating!" says Trinity.

They turn to me.

"Really? I can still barely find my way back to my house from school!"

"Great," says Trinity, slapping her arms at her sides. "I'm starting to understand how those kids got stuck out here, and I don't think it had anything to do with Forest Protectors. They were just as dumb as we are."

But as the wind begins to kick up, choosing a direction—any direction—takes on a new urgency.

"I say right," Enzo hollers over the wind.

"Right it is!" I say, and we lean into the wind and the rain, vines still doing their best to scrape our shins.

All at once, I'm aware of a new sound, one even more worrying than the thunder and the wind. Suddenly, there's a low groan coming from behind us . . . or maybe from the side. It's impossible to place, but one thing is certain: The sound isn't human.

"Guys?" I say, and the other two stop, turning to see my expression before hearing the sound themselves.

"MOVE!" Trinity screams, pushing Enzo. I back away in the other direction, my foot slipping on a pile of leaves as I tumble backward and down a steep embankment.

I tumble just long enough to see the tree come down, its skinny trunk unable to withstand the violent winds of the storm.

Then I hit a skid and roll, somersaulting and feeling the jagged edge of something rake a long scratch down my back.

When I land, I'm on my stomach, facedown in the mud, fully unprotected by the tree line. I've come to a stop at the bottom of the hill and into a clearing.

I come to my senses a little too slowly, and I spring to my feet searching for the falling tree above. Luckily, it must have hit the ground higher up, or I would have been about a thousand years too late to miss being squashed.

Which reminds me . . .

"Enzo! Trinity!" I yell, but I can hardly hear my own voice over the wind, let alone expect them to hear me. Dread coats my stomach as I consider where the tree might have landed—if it could have landed on them.

"They got out of the way," I say to myself. "They got out of the way in time."

But I don't know that for sure, and even though the scrape on my back is burning and I have mud up my nose, I peer through the rain for any way out of the forest: an overgrown path, the hint of a signpost, anything.

Then, at the far end of the clearing, I see my first evidence of civilization since we entered the forest. It looks to be a wooden pole about hip height. I run across the clearing, feeling weirdly exposed away from the trees. When I reach the pole, I see it marks what was likely once a path, though this path is even more obscured than the one at the top of the embankment.

"I've never wanted a machete more," I say to myself, and I have to laugh because when have I ever wanted a machete?

I form my hand into a little blade, my thumb tucked against my palm, and push my way through the overgrown trail, resigning myself to the curse of three leaves.

I expect to find myself in another clearing at the end of the path. What I don't expect is a relay tower.

"What?"

It's almost as if someone planted seeds, and a relay tower sprouted up in the middle of the forest. I can't see the top of it from where I stand, but I can see the wall of a small outbuilding in its shadow. I follow the wall, high grass pressing against it and eroding the wood near the foundation. The wind is so strong now, it's blowing the rain sideways, flickering in my ear and shooting into my eyes. I put my head down as much as I can so I can still see where I'm going, but mostly, I'm holding on to the wall for guidance.

Then my hand finds the end of the wall, and I turn with it, walking a few more steps before finally finding a surface that's metal.

It's the knob of a door.

"Could I be this lucky?" I say, and of course not. It's locked.

You could just . . .

"No," I tell the voice in my head that would love nothing more than to turn me into a full-blown vandal. "I'm not a criminal."

Oh no? Then why do you still carry your lockpicks every-where?

And really, is it that much different than picking locks in our apartment building in Germany? In our new house in Raven Brooks?

The rain has soaked through my clothes. I can feel the kit pressing against me in my pocket.

"It's breaking and entering," I say to the voice.

You're right. Death by pneumonia or bird people is way better.

But it isn't the voice that convinces me to slide the kit from my back pocket and fumble the pick out of the slot and into the keyhole.

It's the sound of a single footfall landing on a twig some-where nearby.

Somehow, the footstep cut through all the crashing of the storm, just to let me know it was nearby. Just to let me know I was being followed.

"Enzo?" I call, but either I'm not loud enough or it's not Enzo.

My hands shake as I twitch the pick in the lock, clumsily searching for the catch while I listen for another footfall. It doesn't take long before I do.

My hands shake harder, and I drop the pick I was using in the grass.

"Get it together," I say under my breath, casting a quick glance over my shoulder. I can't tell if the trees are moving from the wind or from . . .

Forest Protectors.

"Shut up," I tell myself and pull a different pick from the kit—any pick, it doesn't matter. I'd jam a screwdriver in there at this point. Whatever it takes to break the lock off.

By some miracle, I feel the catch despite all my gracelessness. I practically fall through the metal door, but when I turn to lock it from the inside, I see that I've done exactly what I feared and broken the lock.

The building is dark and small, and I have to slide my hands along the wall on the inside just like I did on the outside. I thought it would be better to get out of the rain, but the sudden silence is unnerving.

Except it's not exactly silent because I can still hear the wind from outside slamming against the building, making the internal workings of this place moan under the strain. It gives off the impression that the whole place is alive.

That's maybe the worst thought you've ever had, Aaron. Nice work.

I should be taking it slower than I am, but I'm not about to stay near the door with the broken lock and wait to see if whatever was in the forest manages to find its way in.

I press both my hands to the wall now, desperate for another doorknob or at least a light switch.

The floor is slick and uneven, and the air is cold, even colder because I'm completely soaked. My shirt and my pants are holding tight to me like they're terrified, too. I'm shaking all over, and whether it's from the cold or abject terror, I'm having a hard time walking under all this trembling.

After another few minutes of stumbling every three feet, I make myself stop, pressing against the wall and balling my hands into fists just so I can hold still long enough to take a few deep breaths. I haven't heard the door open yet, but I'm sure I would have heard it in this small place, so all I need to do is hang out here and wait for the worst of the storm to pass.

Then you can sprint home like your life depends on it. Because it just mi—

"Don't," I scold the incredibly unhelpful voice in my head.

Then, after one more deep breath, I lean to my right and, my back still pressed against the cold wall, prepare to move farther down what I can only guess is some sort of corridor, when all at once, I fall through an opening in the wall.

Instead of stumbling into emptiness, my arm catches what feels like a table leg, and I buckle over something else that finds my middle, knocking the wind out of me before I finally trip and land on the floor.

Graceful as always.

Groaning, I find my way back to my feet and stare around the room until my eyes have a chance to adjust to the new level of darkness in here. I risk another step, and almost immediately, my foot kicks something over that sounds like it could be made of metal.

Crouching, I hook my fingers around a handle and feel my way to the bottom of a camping lantern. A stash of battery-operated lanterns was one of the few treasures Mya and I found in the storage crevices of our apartment building in Germany. I assume the landlord kept them in case of power outages, but Mya and I used them for basically everything *other* than emergencies. We lighted forts with them in our rooms and placed them strategically throughout the apartment, pretending to be agents of international espionage. We rolled them under our beds when we couldn't sleep and read or drew instead.

I feel for the tiny key dial and turn it, watching as the yellow glow from the lantern floods a spot on the floor. When I hold it up, I quickly realize I'm in an office full of abandoned furniture, filing cabinets, and various sharp objects and gadgets for which I couldn't begin to guess a use.

What's weirder is that it's like the storm that's raging outside right now somehow made its way in here years ago, because this place is covered in dust and broken parts. File folders are torn apart and dumped into a mottled pile in a corner. Wooden chairs that once probably stood around a small table in the corner of the room are snapped into pieces, their jagged edges pointing to the ceiling. The desk I whacked my arm on still stands stoically in the middle of the room near the door, but everything on top of it has been torn apart, water damaged, or crumpled beyond recognition. A filing cabinet lies on its side along the opposite wall, its drawers emptied and sticking out like tongues.

Then there's what remains on the walls: a painting of some sort of country setting, all green smears of bushes and fields dotted with poppies. There's a worn topographic map of what I'm guessing must be the city limits of Raven Brooks and maybe more. There's a chalkboard whose writings have long since been erased.

There's a side-by-side frame holding two degrees from the university: one for Roger A. and one for Adelle R. Peterson.

"No way," I whisper, because it couldn't possibly be that I've managed to stumble straight into an office that used to be occupied by my Very Important grandparents who no one will talk about.

If the university degrees weren't enough to convince me, though, the overturned picture on top of the desk is.

It's yellowed and dislodged from its broken frame, curling at the edges without protection behind the glass. There's no mistaking it's them—despite the wedding attire, they wear almost identical expressions in the picture that hangs in their house. The house that's now ours.

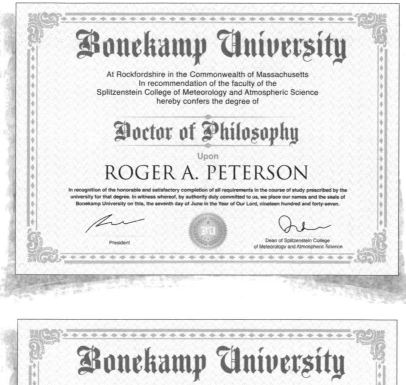

Bonekamp University

At Rockfordshire in the Commonwealth of Massachusetts
In recommendation of the faculty of the
Splitzenstein College of Meteorology and Atmospheric Science
hereby confers the degree of

Doctor of Philosophy

Upon

ROGER A. PETERSON

In recognition of the honorable and satisfactory completion of all requirements in the course of study prescribed by the university for that degree. In witness whereof, by authority duly committed to us, we place our names and the seals of Bonekamp University on this, the seventh day of June in the Year of Our Lord, nineteen hundred and forty-seven.

President

Dean of Splitzenstein College
of Meteorology and Atmospheric Science

Bonekamp University

At Rockfordshire in the Commonwealth of Massachusetts
In recommendation of the faculty of the
Splitzenstein College of Meteorology and Atmospheric Science
hereby confers the degree of

Doctor of Philosophy

Upon

ADELLE R. PETERSON

In recognition of the honorable and satisfactory completion of all requirements in the course of study prescribed by the university for that degree. In witness whereof, by authority duly committed to us, we place our names and the seals of Bonekamp University on this, the seventh day of June in the Year of Our Lord, nineteen hundred and forty-seven.

President

Dean of Splitzenstein College
of Meteorology and Atmospheric Science

I'm just about to go back to wondering what the heck this building is when I hear the sound I'd almost forgotten to fear: the door.

It creaks on its hinge exactly the way it did after I picked the lock and slammed it shut, right before I realized I'd broken the lock off.

Now I hear it shut again. I hear the footsteps that follow.

Whatever feeling had returned to my body after I warmed up drains out of me now, and it takes everything I have to overcome the paralysis that's set in. There's exactly one hiding place in this room: behind the overturned table in the far corner.

Which would mean I'm literally cornered.

Panic leaves me undecided for too long, and all at once, the footsteps have gained speed, traveling down the dark corridor at an alarming rate. I don't have any choice but to stay in the office and hide.

Practically leaping over the table, I crouch behind it, remembering too late that I left the lantern glowing in the middle of the room.

When the footsteps come to a stop, they're just outside the office.

There's only one reason someone would be here—whoever is here saw me come in. Whoever is here *followed* me.

My heart pounds hard enough to hurt my chest, and for a second, the room grows dark and I think maybe the lantern went out. Then I realize it isn't the room that's gone black. It's my vision. My eyes are shut tight.

A footfall echoes inside the room where I struggle to stay conscious, but I might as well pass out. If a bird person is about to kill me, maybe it would make the pecking hurt less.

Another footfall, and I listen for talons tapping on the linoleum.

Another footfall, and was that the rustle of feathers?

Another footfall, and this is the end. This is where I think my last thought, where I draw my last breath. No one even knows where I am.

Then, I hear the creak of the handle on the lantern, and suddenly the light lifts.

Right over my head.

CHAPTER 6

The light swings high overhead. Each time it rocks back and forth, it casts a grotesque shadow on the wall, and I won't scream. I refuse to scream.

Instead, I whimper.

"Well, I see you've got your father's knack for mischief."

I try to place the voice. Can bird people talk?

"Though I don't remember him having a talent for lockpicking. Truth be told, that was more up my alley."

When the light finally steadies on the wall, I brace myself and look up from my crouch to find Mr. Gershowitz, his lanky body casting one long shadow. Seeing him here, grinning in the lantern light, the room no longer looks quite so ominous.

Except that I still can't stop my body from shaking.

"C'mon," he says, extending his hand down to me. "I'll answer your questions if you answer mine."

I take his hand without hesitating. I have zero idea of where I am or why Mr. Gershowitz is here, but if there's a single certainty I have, it's that Mr. Gershowitz is a good person. Dad wouldn't be friends with him otherwise.

"I'll go first," Mr. Gershowitz says, making sure I'm steady on my feet before swapping out the lantern for his own flashlight. Only then do I see that he's wearing a uniform, a badge stitched to the front of his shirt.

He points to the badge. "Private security," he says. "Raven Brooks City Council likes a little extra vigilance."

He leaves his explanation there. It seems to be enough. Dad did say his friend works nights.

"Okay, my turn," he says, keeping the beam of his flashlight pointed away from my eyes. "What in the name of bacon are you doing out here on a night like this all alone?"

"Bacon?" I say.

"Do your folks know you're here?"

"Where is 'here' exactly?"

"Are you one of those kids who answers questions with questions? I don't do well with those kinds of kids."

"Sorry," I say, and I really am. "It's just that I thought you were . . ."

He eyes me closely.

Tell him. Tell him you thought he was one of the bird people here to peck your eyes out and make a nest from your hair.

"I was trying to get out of the rain," I say, choosing about ten percent of the truth. "My friends and I got split up."

Mr. Gershowitz eyes me for another second, then seems to accept my story, or at least gets tired of questioning it.

"Rain's mostly stopped now. Let me walk you home."

I want to play it cool, but it's impossible to act like I'm anything but thrilled that I won't have to cut through the woods alone.

Mr. Gershowitz leaves the office first, giving me one last chance to look around at whatever's left of my grandparents' workplace.

When I turn back around, Mr. Gershowitz is already gone, and I must turn the wrong way because I make it two steps before he stops me with his light.

"Not that way!" he yells, even though I've barely gone anywhere. I jump at his tone, trying to see his expression, but I can't get a good look, thanks to the glare from the flashlight.

"Sorry, I—"

"Stay close. Don't go wandering," he scolds, and I'm starting to feel a little less grateful.

He takes me out of the building, and even though the thunder is still rumbling in the distance and some of the wind is still kicking up the leaves, the storm has mostly passed.

Once we've moved a little farther away from the building, I sneak another look at the tower over my shoulder.

"It's a weather station," he says, picking his way through a mostly obscured path. This trail is definitely not the same way I came. Of course, to retrace *that* path, I'd have to roll back up the embankment.

A weather station. Okay, so that makes sense, I guess. Mr. Donaldson had said my grandparents were famous for their work in geology and meteorology. What doesn't make sense is why everyone is acting like that's some sort of crime.

"Sounds kinda boring," I say to Mr. Gershowitz, prodding for more information.

He seems to understand because he says, "In any other town, maybe."

"You knew them, right?"

Mr. Gershowitz slows his pace so we can walk side by side, and I catch him eyeing me before he turns his gaze ahead to the trail, the light from his flashlight bobbing.

"Your grandparents? A little. Only enough to thank them when they had me over for dinner, which was more often than it should have been. My parents worked long hours . . . couldn't always put food on the table at a normal hour."

He's trying to say a nice thing about my grandparents, but I can tell he's starting to get uncomfortable. I guess that's why I push a little harder. I'm getting tired of secrets.

"I think people were afraid of them."

Mr. Gershowitz loses his footing, and I catch his elbow before he goes down on the slick path.

He mutters a thank-you before righting himself. He's quiet for another minute before he starts walking.

Then he says, "You ever seen a meteor shower?"

It's possibly the most random question anyone has ever asked me.

"Um, no?"

"It's magnificent," he says. "And it's terrifying. The light is so bright, you think it's going to scatter across the whole sky. Then the dark just . . . swallows it up. Just like that, it's gone."

I get the sense he's trying to tell me something meaningful, but unless my grandparents were astronomers *and* meteorologists, I'm clueless.

Mr. Gershowitz must sense this on some level because he goes on to say, "Sometimes the things that burn the brightest are the scariest right before they flame out. Your grandparents . . . they were the type of people who burned bright."

Clarity drops on me like a house.

They burned bright, just like my dad. And when they were at their brightest—their most genius—they scared him.

They scared everyone.

Mr. Gershowitz has known my dad for a long time. It's impossible to believe he hasn't seen that same spark in him.

"Your grandparents wanted to put Raven Brooks on the map. In a lot of ways, they did. And in a lot of ways, it was good for the town," he says, tiptoeing around the topic the same way he sidesteps the uneven ground.

"But?" I say. Because there's obviously a "but."

"Some people weren't looking for that sort of attention."

"Like who?"

I've crossed into forbidden territory. I can tell by the way he pinches his mouth shut now. Mr. Gershowitz is done talking. It makes me wonder if he was one of the ones who didn't want that sort of attention. It makes me wonder if maybe taking him up on his offer to walk me home was more dangerous than I'd realized.

Then, as fast as the thought comes to mind, it leaves, because he says, "Your dad isn't like them."

He stops walking, so I'm forced to stop, too. He looks at me, making sure I look back. "In case you were wondering."

I don't know how he knew, but he did, and I'm not sure I could ever tell him how much it means, saying that one little thing. I'm not sure I could ever thank Mr. Gershowitz enough for that.

When we start walking again, I try to turn the conversation in a safer direction. "I thought they only worked at home. How come no one ever talks about this place?"

Mr. Gershowitz shakes his head. "Not really sure. They just stopped working out of this place at some point, started moving everything to the house."

He could have stopped there, but he added, almost too quietly for me to hear, "Paranoia's a funny thing."

Honestly, I didn't need that last part.

"You said you and your friends got split up. Shouldn't've been out here in the first place," he says.

I know I should apologize or explain or do something to tell him he's right, but Mr. Gershowitz and I seem to be in this weird place where we can say anything and none of it is out of bounds, so I try my luck.

"You work out here a lot," I say instead of ask. When he's quiet, I keep going. "Have you ever seen anything . . . weird in the woods?"

He's still quiet. I'm dying to keep asking questions, but something inside me tells me to shut up and wait.

"No," he says, and nothing more.

By the time I start to recognize the path we're walking, I

realize we've made it back to the place we were standing right around the time I lost Enzo and Trinity. I wish I'd been paying closer attention to the way we came.

Not that I'm in any hurry to get back to these woods anytime soon.

We finally break through a clearing in the trees, and we're out of the forest, but not in the same place I entered. Apparently, there's another way, one that doesn't involve cutting through alleyways and dodging poison ivy.

After about five blocks of walking mostly in silence, we pass by the natural grocer, and I finally have my bearings.

Only now it occurs to me that I have no idea what Mr. Gershowitz is going to say to my parents about where I've been or why I'm soaked and scraped and probably still have twigs in my hair.

Or why the streetlights are on and I'm only just now coming home.

No matter how hard I try, though, I can't work up the nerve to ask Mr. Gershowitz just how much of the truth he's going to tell.

Mom's on top of me the second I open the front door. Dad isn't far behind.

"Practically eight o'clock!" Mom says, skipping to the important part while she holds my face and examines every inch of me for damage.

"And with the storm," my dad adds, grabbing a towel from the bathroom to drape over my shoulders.

"And your friends saying they couldn't find you—" Mom says, squeezing my arms, I guess to see if I have broken any bones.

"I'll call their parents," says my dad.

Mya is peeking around the corner of the kitchen looking betrayed, like she thought I'd left her and wasn't coming back.

I get it, everyone. The woods was a bad idea.

Only after my dad returns from the kitchen, having hung up with both sets of parents, does anyone seem to notice that Mr. Gershowitz is standing right next to me, not saying a word.

Dad is the one to finally say something.

"You found him?" he asks, his big hand resting on his friend's shoulder. The look of relief in Dad's eyes makes me feel a new level of horrible. He's about to find out I had them worried because I just had to be *the cool new kid who wasn't afraid of some stupid forest.*

But Mr. Gershowitz surprises me.

"He made it out of the woods all by himself. I found him near the natural grocer. Poor kid's probably starving." Then he laughed. "You'd have to be to eat the food from that place."

He doesn't even flinch at the lie. He just casually omits that I was breaking and entering, creeping around the forbidden tomb of my grandparents' research.

Mom shudders. "That woman."

Mr. Gershowitz laughs again.

Dad searches his friend's face. If anyone can sniff out an untruth, it's Dad. But his face relaxes into an easy smile soon enough, and just like that, I'm off the hook.

Well, with everyone but Mya.

Upstairs, she gets ready for bed and doesn't even say good night. I have to be the one to knock on her door, and even then, she only lets me in grudgingly.

"You went without me," she says, holding her rag doll to her chest and playing with its hair so she doesn't have to look at me.

"It was just a stupid forest," I say.

But that's not what she means. She means that I did something that was *dangerous*. She means that she thought I might not come back.

That I'd left her alone.

I want to tell her what I found, about the office and Grandma and Grandpa, and the urban legend of the Forest Protectors. I want to tell her all of it.

But everything still feels blurry. I can't make sense of any of it. How could I possibly expect Mya to?

Instead, I tell her I'm sorry and wait for her to accept my apology.

And because it's Mya, she does. In her own way, that is.

"You smell. Get out of my room."

Long after I should have taken the shower I obviously need and gone to bed for the sleep I need just as badly, I find myself instead in the basement, staring at my painted sunshine and a blank pad of paper. I had plans to draw the office in the weather station before I forgot all of the details, but now that I'm here, once again, my hand doesn't seem to be able to capture what my brain is telling it.

I was just remembering that I never thanked Mr. Gershowitz for . . . well, for everything, when suddenly I hear his voice. Not in the basement but echoing from another part of the house. I probably wouldn't have heard him at all, but his voice sounds agitated, and it's followed by my dad's muffled voice over top of it. It doesn't take me long to understand that they're arguing.

"That's not what I'm saying," I can hear Mr. Gershowitz say, but my dad's voice is deeper, and it rolls right over him.

"I know how to protect my family."

"Ted, listen to me. You haven't been out there—I have. I'm telling you, things are happening. Strange things, like before—"

"That doesn't mean—"

"Your boy's even starting to ask questions, about his grand-parents, the forest, the—"

"What did you tell him?"

For just a second, the blood in my body stops flowing. I've never heard Dad's voice sound like that. Even through the vent, I can hear something's changed. All of a sudden, he isn't Dad. He's menacing, cold, like he's momentarily slipped out of his own body. I can't see him, but I can imagine his eyes clearly. Like icy green holes with tiny black pinpoint pupils.

"Nothing, Ted. I didn't tell him a thing," Mr. Gershowitz says so quietly, I almost don't hear him at all.

Everything goes quiet for what feels like an eternity. I start to think maybe they've left the room, but then I hear my dad talk again.

"I think it's time for you to go, Ike."

More silence.

I didn't think footsteps could sound like anything other than footsteps. But if I had to assign Mr. Gershowitz's footsteps a feeling just then, it would be reluctance. He doesn't want to go. At least not like this.

But hearing Dad's voice turn so cold, there isn't a person alive who would feel like they could stay.

I wish I could run up the stairs and pull Mr. Gershowitz back—to tell him that I'll listen. Whatever my dad won't let him say, I will. I'll hear it all. I won't say a word. Just as long as he can take some of these secrets away from me.

Instead, I stand at the foot of the stairs in the basement and listen as the front door above opens with a tiny creak, then closes after a delay, like he was giving my dad one more chance to change his mind and invite him back in.

I stay in the basement for a long time, long enough to hear my dad leave his office and trudge up the stairs, closing himself behind his bedroom door with my mom and leaving me to find my own way back.

CHAPTER 7

Mya and I are running. It's the worst day to be late.

"It was your turn to set the alarm," Mya says between gulps of breath. Her backpack is bouncing against her, shoving her forward with every stride.

"Reason number five thousand to GET YOUR OWN ALARM CLOCK," I pant back, looking quickly right and left before pulling her across the street and rounding the corner.

"I told you, mine got broken in the move," she says, but she's a horrible liar.

"Yeah, sure."

"We're going to miss the bus," says Mya, and about this, she might be right. And about this, I might not be too brokenhearted.

It's field-trip day, and we've all been warned that the bus will leave promptly at eight forty-five. Miss the bus and you'll miss the Golden Apple factory tour.

It would also mean missing a glimpse at the forest I have zero interest in seeing again after the last time.

"We'll make it," I say, picking up a tiny bit of speed so she thinks I'm at least trying.

It's eight fifty when we do finally make it to school. I think for sure I've dodged the field trip, but there's Trinity, waving to us from the bottom step of the bus, hanging out of it like a train conductor.

"C'mon, you guys!"

Mya yanks my arm, and we board the bus to find a bazillion other kids squirming and shouting, along with a handful of annoyed-looking teachers, chaperones, and a bus driver who looks even sleepier than I do.

"I convinced them to wait," Trinity says, pulling me by the arm and seating me next to Enzo all the way in the back. Mya shoves in beside Maritza and Lucy toward the front.

"It's the least we could do," Trinity says in explanation of why she pleaded with the teachers to hold the bus.

"We feel bad," says Enzo.

"Really bad," says Trinity.

"Like, the worst bad," says Enzo.

"Guys, it's fi—"

"What happened to you?"

"We thought we heard you yelling, but—"

"Your parents probably hate us. Do they hate us?"

"GUYS!" I yell, making at least a few heads turn.

I try to smile until everyone goes about their business, then look at Enzo and Trinity again. "I'm fine."

"We're just . . . don't hate us, okay?" says Trinity, and Enzo nods enthusiastically.

"What, just because you left me to die in a forest full of blood-thirsty bird people?" I say, and Trinity's eyes widen in horror.

"Whoa, I'm joking!" I say, and Enzo laughs, but Trinity still looks more traumatized than I am.

I'm not going to lie. It feels pretty great to have friends who actually think *I* might hate *them*.

It almost feels good enough for me to forget that we're going to a factory that's completely surrounded by the woods they left me in. Almost.

"Oh hey, I nearly forgot, there's something I need to talk to you about," says Enzo as we get off the bus, but the second Trinity gets too far ahead, I've lost him again.

The factory road is set far from the wilds of the forest, though I can't help but feel I'm developing some sort of phobia of trees. But once we leave the bus and go inside the factory, it's a completely different world.

For one glorious moment, we aren't thinking about how lame it is to be on a field trip with elementary-schoolers. We aren't worried about strategically placing ourselves in line so we can be close—but not too close—to our crushes. We don't care about what we look like, what we smell like, what we sound like. We're in the midst of candy. Glorious, cavity-making, blood sugar–rising, ecstasy-inducing candy.

There's a moment of silence.

Then it's madness.

"All right, all *right*, everyone!" hollers Mr. Donaldson, and for the most part, we get it together again. Enzo puts himself as close to Trinity as possible without looking completely desperate. I try to time the movements of the factory workers to see how difficult it would be to slip into the tasting room. Mya and Maritza and Lucy link arms so they don't get separated in the crowd. Trinity takes notes.

"And over here is the taffy pull," says the tour guide who could just as easily be guiding us through the Smithsonian for as seriously as he takes the Golden Apple legacy. He is suited in head-to-toe Golden Apple paraphernalia, which until today I didn't know existed. I'm guessing no one did. There's a red vest and matching red pants, a pin-striped suit jacket with piping along the collar. His black shoes shine so brightly under the factory floor lights, I have to look away. But the best thing about our guide—aside from his folksy name, Mr. Pippin—is his apple-shaped beret. The little loop at the top of the hat forms the stem of the apple, and this man is all business about his beret and every other part of him.

"Children, this way please. Single file, please. *Children!*" he calls to us, making me cringe each time.

He's ushering us through the chocolate room, and I'm so blissed out right now, I can barely keep my head together. A quick look at the "children" around me tells me I'm not alone. You can almost smell the euphoria.

"Hands at our sides, please," says Mr. Pippin over the hum of the cocoa nib grinder. I actively have to keep from drooling.

Mr. Pippin takes us through a winding maze of upper-level corridors, identical doors leading to offices and back-office departments, each alive with the hustle and bustle of the daily activities of the factory.

"Don't worry," he says, "We'll be back to the fun part in a moment."

When we emerge from the corridors, we're standing on a

metal balcony overlooking the main factory floor. Hundreds of workers in plastic hair nets and gloves sort Golden Apples along a giant conveyer belt, moving with enough speed to fill—

"—five hundred boxes of Golden Apples a day," says Mr. Pippin. "Yes, young lady in the back?"

I hear Maritza's voice shout confidently over the noise of machinery.

"What sort of profit margins are you operating on?"

Mr. Pippin takes a moment to absorb her question. To be fair, I think we all do. All except for Enzo. He looks entirely unsurprised.

"What a . . . what an advanced question from such a young mind!" says Mr. Pippin, though he doesn't sound impressed so much as annoyed.

"Have you measured transverse flexibility in the rigidity of the conveyer belt?" asks Lucy.

"Um . . . well, we—"

"Is your maintenance schedule open to the public?" asks Mya.

"Oh, good point. That would give great insight into the margins," Lucy agrees enthusiastically.

Mr. Pippin blinks at Mr. Donaldson. "Sorry, how old did you say—?"

"Why don't we save our questions until the end of the tour?" says Mr. Donaldson, sounding so exhausted I wonder how he's still standing.

I've never seen a person look more relieved than Mr. Pippin.

"Excellent idea. Yes, questions at the end, children."

And away we go to the "History Room," which is basically a room filled with old, framed pictures and newspaper articles, and a handful of pedestals scattered through the middle of the room housing old candy wrappers under glass cases.

The origins of the Golden Apple dynasty.

"And over here, you'll see how it all started," says Mr. Pippin, his reverence for the Golden Apple Origins almost religious.

The origins, as it turns out, are actually kind of interesting. Apparently, Golden Apples started as a mistake, when Florence Dewitt (or Gammy Flo, as Mr. Pippin calls her, which earns him a collective eye roll) accidentally poured chocolate over her truffles too soon, making the chocolate melt in with the caramel instead of forming a hard coating over it. When she came back to check on the truffles, they'd all melted into little pools in shapes that looked like apples.

From there, Gammy Flo, like so many other accidental entrepreneurs, started selling her Golden Apples out of her kitchen, at bake sales, the county fair. Along came the Tavishes, this über-rich family who thought Gammy Flo was sitting on a gold mine, so to speak, and dumped a bunch of money in her lap. The Golden Apple Corporation was born, and presumably, Gammy Flo died happy and rich.

The Tavishes suddenly became very important in Raven Brooks, as most rich people who make towns richer do. Mr. Pippin talks about them like they're important, too. He acts like they invented candy. Like, *candy in general.*

Enzo appears beside me and elbows me deep in the ribs.

"This is what I wanted to tell you about," he says.

"You want to tell me about boring old people with lots of money?"

"Kind of, yeah."

Mr. Pippin clears his throat at the interruption, and Mr. Donaldson mimes a lip zip from the side of the room at us.

"Now, if you'll come this way, I think the next room—our Vision Room—is what you're all going to be most interested in seeing," says Mr. Pippin, and I have my doubts.

As the rest of the group files out of the room obediently, I linger: a framed headline from one of the articles hanging on the wall has caught my eye.

"Make waves," I mutter to myself. I know who the article is talking about before I even reach the end of the headline.

Sure enough, there in the first paragraph is mention of Roger

and Adelle Peterson, and their Very Important work at the university, paid for in large part by the Very Important Tavish family.

On the brink of fiscal disaster, the university study—itself a mystery but for the highest level of involvement—has been revived by a sizeable donation from local benefactor the Tavish Society, a charitable foundation developed and maintained by the illustrious Tavish family.

Says Raven Brooks University President Beaumont M. Reginald, "We're exceedingly grateful to the Tavish Society for their generosity and dedication to scientific advancement."

I keep scanning the article for another mention of my grandparents, but all references to the study keep their names conspicuously absent from the record.

Instead, my eye is drawn to another article farther down on the time line—this one with the headline "Golden Apples Get a Second Chance."

Known for its philanthropic spirit, the Tavish Society has announced a donation to rebuild the Golden Apple factory after the destruction of the first factory. While the cause of the fire that reduced the first factory to rubble has been ruled inconclusive, rumors of arson persist as witnesses still claim to have seen two shadowy figures fleeing the scene shortly after the first flames were reported. The Tavish Society's donation came under scrutiny, given that the owners of the factory are the very same Tavishes who run the charitable organization.

I'm so absorbed by the article on the wall, I jump about a foot when I feel a hand close around my wrist.

It's Mya, and she looks more frightened than me, but for a completely different reason.

"You need to see this."

She drags me into the Vision Room, and it's a vision all right.

The first thing I notice is the tracks. Three-dimensional roller-coaster tracks twist and turn across the walls of the room, climbing high and dipping low, a small robotic train moving across the ties with surprising speed. It zips along its track as the younger kids—even some of the older kids—watch with open mouths and wide eyes.

The next thing I see is the garishly painted canopy, scaled to size like the rest of the contents of the room, draped over an amphitheater not unlike the one in Germany where my mom and the other dancers used to perform. There's a scaled model of a concession stand, a ticket booth, a prize booth. There's a model of a carousel, its top just as brightly painted as the canopy. There's a Ferris wheel. There's a fun house and a spinning ride.

I look around at the way every single pair of eyes sparkles at the possibility of this magical amusement park, Golden Apple–themed and set right here in every Raven Brooks kid's backyard.

Filled with dread, I turn to Mya, who looks right back at me the same way. There's no question about it now. No dismissing the words of the grocery store lady Mrs. Tillman, or the contracts and blueprints in my dad's office that he and my mom both tried to hide. There's no denying exactly why it is we're in Raven Brooks.

"He's going to build another one," says Mya quietly, so quietly that even if the room wasn't buzzing with palpable excitement, I would have still struggled to hear her.

All I can do is nod. I want to tell her she's wrong, that she's overreacting, jumping to conclusions. But here's the truth, an entire room dedicated to it, laid out in scaled-model form for us to take in the entire vision of the Golden Apple Corporation.

If that wasn't bad enough, my eyes soon fall on a collage of photographs mounted to the far wall, surrounding the words A LEGACY OF INNOVATION. To my horror, prominently featured in the Vision Room is a tribute to Dad's amusement park designs, his most daring and terrifying rides pictured with joyous parkgoers, their arms raised, their faces frozen in screams as they travel the course my dad built for their enjoyment. It should be something I'm proud of. Mya and I should be relishing the attention placed on our dad and his accomplishments.

Instead, I watch every ounce of color drain from Mya's face. I feel the tips of my fingers go cold, then numb. Because each of those parks has a disaster tied to it, from the fun house at Bosco Bay to the flume ride at Fernweh Welt.

At the head of the room, Mr. Donaldson leans into Mr. Pippin's ear, and Mr. Pippin's eyes grow to the size of quarters.

"Attention! Attention, children!" Mr. Pippin says, I guess to all of us? "It appears we are in the presence of genius!"

"No," Mya whispers.

"Please don't," I mouth.

But it's too late.

"Not only is the famous Theodore Masters Peterson heading up the design of the Golden Apple Amusement Park, but his son and daughter are right here among us!"

I know Mr. Pippin is expecting everyone to *ooh* and *ahh* the way he does, but what happens instead is every head turns to Mya and me, confused as to why Mr. Pippin is so excited, and why Mya and I look so pale.

Mr. Pippin laughs. "Now, don't worry. We won't ask you to reveal any secrets about the big ride," he says.

At first, his mention of secrets is all I can focus on. The word ricochets off the walls of my brain, and I'm pretty much just wishing it would knock me unconscious.

Then the rest of what Mr. Pippin said sinks in.

"Big ride?"

"Well, of course," says Mr. Pippin, turning his gaze to the rest of the room, clearly happy to once again have a captive audience.

"We've asked Mr. Peterson to create a very special ride, something one of a kind that only visitors of the Golden Apple Amusement Park can enjoy. And Mr. Peterson has accepted that challenge. He's sworn to secrecy until opening day, of course."

"Of course," I whisper.

Mya looks like she might faint, and I discretely hold on to her arm to keep her steady. Not sure who's going to keep *me* steady, though.

Then, Maritza swoops in to save us from the weight of this new burden.

"Will the secret ride be a large part of your marketing strategy?"

"And how will safety checks be made public?" adds Lucy.

Some of the color returns to Mya's face as Mr. Pippin's own face turns sort of purplish.

"I really don't know," he says, sounding defeated.

"Oooh, could we talk to your head of engineering?" says Lucy as they corner Mr. Pippin with the enthusiasm only weirdly smart elementary-schoolers can possess. Whatever embarrassment we have to endure in this moment, at least it's clear Mya has truly found her people.

I'm just starting to wonder if I have, too, when Enzo stumbles toward me, tipping one of the display pillars and catching it before it goes crashing to the ground. From the corner of my eye, I see Mr. Pippin gasp dramatically.

Trinity joins us from across the room.

"Did you show him yet?" she asks Enzo.

"Just getting to that," he says, pulling a piece of paper with a frayed left edge from his pocket and unfolding it on the floor while we crowd around it. It appears Enzo has gotten over his inability to function around Trinity. I can't help but feel a twinge of pride at the part I played in that.

"Take a look at this," he says to me, pointing to a black-and-white picture of some stuffy-looking people I now recognize as the wealthy members of the Tavish family.

"Hang on, did you . . . is this from a textbook?" I say, recognizing the distinctive page border from Mrs. Ryland's geography class. "Did you deface school property?" I chide him, *tsking* and shaking my head slowly.

"In pursuit of a greater good. Would you get serious for a second?"

I nod. "Boring old people. Got it."

Enzo gives me a look. "Not at the picture. What's *next to* the picture."

I crouch to the floor with him and skim the text beside the photo. Sure enough, I quickly catch sight of my own last name.

One ongoing study, funded by the Tavish Society and facilitated by husband-and-wife-geological/meteorological-sciences team Adelle and Roger Peterson, aims to shed light on the unexplained magnetic properties detected in various latitudes of their hometown. While little is known about the study or its methodology, the fact remains that private donors are increasingly relied upon for scientific advancement.

I shrug. "Okay, so my grandparents are textbook-famous."

"Who's famous?" Mya asks, making her way over to see what we're all crowded around. Lucy is still chatting up Mr. Pippin, but Maritza is close behind.

"Your grandparents," says Trinity, and Mya's eyes shift to me.

"According to Enzo, they were working on a project no one knows about thanks to money they got from old people," I say.

"You ripped that out of a textbook?" asks Maritza, scandalized.

"Would you forget about the textbook? You're missing the point," Enzo says to Maritza, to me, to the room in general because at the moment, he's clearly the only one connecting the dots.

"Do you know what the copyright on that book is?" he says.

"Um, no. But I take it you—"

"Nineteen sixty-one," Enzo interrupts me. "Don't you see what that means?"

"That our textbooks are in desperate need of updating," says Maritza.

"No, I mean yes, but what it really means is that for the first time ever, we know what your grandparents were working on and when!"

Enzo looks around, waiting for all of us—or even just one of us—to understand the significance of his discovery. We are all failing him.

He sighs. His shoulders fall. "By nineteen sixty, your grandparents had gone completely off the grid. People rarely even saw them. Everyone knew they were working on something big, but no one knew what that was."

He slaps his index finger down on the textbook page. "But someone knew. The Tavish Society."

"Oh," I say.

"Oh?" Enzo says, indignant. "That's it?"

No, that's not it. Not even close, but I can't exactly say that this isn't how I wanted to find out about my grandparents . . . with a crowd around to witness it. If they were hiding something, and it sure seems like they were, it's a fun mystery to everyone else. To me, it's one more secret to protect.

Because even if I could learn every one of my grandparents' secrets, I'm starting to feel more and more like I don't want to. If I could go back to that day at Fernweh Welt and run the opposite direction of the flume ride, I would. There are some things that you can't unsee. Some horrible secrets that you're better off not knowing.

So instead, I say, "It's cool, Enzo. I mean, what you found is super interesting. But it's not like anyone's gonna be able to figure out what my grandparents were doing thirty years ago."

Instead of turning Enzo off the idea, though, this only fans the flames under him.

"See, that's where you're wrong," he says. "It *is* interesting because a whole bunch of other weird stuff was going on around the same time that your grandparents were working on their secret project."

My stomach drops to the floor. I look over at Mya, and she's looking like she wants to find the emergency brake on this speeding train, but what are we supposed to do? Enzo's already full throttle on this. I guess when you're a person who has nothing to hide, you can get excited about mysteries.

"And," Enzo says, because apparently he's not done obliviously ruining my life, "I brought the idea to my dad, and he wants *me* to investigate and write up a piece for the *Banner!*"

"Enzo, that's so great!" says Trinity, and Enzo's ears go pink.

"Way to go, dork," says Maritza, smiling at her brother. "Oooh, do you think Dad would want other stories from kids? We're starting a young inventor's club."

"Sure, I don't see why not," says Enzo. "He's amped about starting this whole section for student reporters in the paper."

Then Enzo turns to me, clapping a hand on my shoulder. "I have you to thank for the idea, you know," he says.

"You do?" says Mya, shifting an accusatory gaze my way.

"No, you don't," I say to Enzo. "No, he doesn't," I say to Mya.

"Sure, I do!" says Enzo. "If it weren't for your suggestion that I go to my dad about writing a story, I never would have considered it."

"Wow," I say. "That's great. I'm such a genius."

"Yeah, brilliant," says Mya like she wants to throw something at me. I can't blame her. *I* want to throw something at me.

"Anyway, my dad said he'd help me with some of the research," says Enzo. "Hey, do you think your dad would be cool with being interviewed?"

"NO!" Mya and I yell together, and everyone stares at us.

"Uh—he's kind of—it's just that he's—"

"He's really busy," Mya says, and at least one of us is thinking fast.

"Yup," I say. "Busy, busy bee. That's Dad."

"Ohhhkaaaay," says Enzo, and for the first time today, I'm suddenly very grateful for Mr. Pippin because he shouts to the room that the tour has concluded. Honestly, I can't tell who's more relieved, Mr. Pippin or me.

"All right," Mr. Donaldson says, bracing himself for whatever he's about to say next. "Let's move on to the candy shop."

"Every kid for themselves!" someone yells.

"Attaaaaack!" someone else roars.

A stampede ensues, and while Enzo, Martiza, Trinity, and Lucy all link arms to stay together, Mya tugs me back by my arm.

"Ow! Hey, we're gonna miss out on the chocolate ones!"

"You're a moron," she says.

"I know," I say.

That's not what she means, though. What she means is she's scared. It's what I mean, too, but I can't let her know that.

"Look, he's going to lose interest in the story the second school gets harder, guaranteed. By the time we have our first quiz, he's going to forget all about our grandparents and whatever else he thinks happened back then."

Mya leans in, looking down while she whispers, "What do *you* think happened? I mean, do you think . . . did they do something bad?"

I swallow hard and hope she doesn't hear the lump that sticks in my throat.

"No way," I say. "Not a chance."

She might know I'm lying. Honestly, part of me would be a little disappointed if she didn't know; she's smarter than that. I think we're both happy to believe the lie, though, at least for a little while.

So, I say it again for emphasis.

144

"Not a chance."

By the time we pile back onto the bus, most of us are buzzing on sugar but otherwise exhausted. Trinity nods off on Enzo's shoulder, and I think he's going to burst with happiness. I think this may have been the best day of his entire life. I wish I could say the same.

*   *   *

Dinner that night is an opportunity. At least that's what I'm choosing to see it as. If I can just get ahead of this story Enzo wants to write by learning that my grandparents were actually pretty boring, I can clear at least this one secret from my vault.

Mya seems to have the same perspective because she's the first one to strike.

"Today was the Golden Apple factory field trip," she says so casually, she actually has me fooled for a minute. Not an ulterior motive in sight.

"Oh, right!" says Mom. "I completely forgot. Did you learn what the Halloween candy is going to be?"

With trick-or-treating season just around the corner, the Golden Apple Corporation has been making a big deal out of unveiling their new mystery candy just in time for the big night. There was some speculation that we'd get a sneak peek on the tour.

"No," says Mya, "but we did get a look at the, um, theme park."

All eyes land on Dad, who manages to cut his chicken without so much as flinching. He's looking at it like he expects it to come alive, though.

"Made that public, have they?" says Dad, casual as can be.

"I think your dad was planning to tell you kids the good news after he'd turned in all of his designs," says Mom diplomatically, but she's approaching with extreme caution. "Right, Ted?"

Dad stays silent. He's just slowly cutting his chicken away from the bone.

"Everyone's really excited you're the one building it," I say. Mya shouldn't have to do all the work. "Especially because, you know, Grandma and Grandpa were such a big deal around here."

I clear my throat. That's what people do when they're speaking normally, right? "What was it you said they used to do again?"

Dad cuts, takes a bite, chews, swallows, cuts. "Don't recall that I did," he says.

It feels stiflingly hot in the kitchen all of a sudden. Did Mom leave the oven on or something?

"Enzo found a passage in his geography textbook about how the Tavish Society was funding their work," says Mya. Not exactly a sly approach, but she's tugging at her shirt collar, so I think she's feeling hot, too.

"Who's Enzo?" says Dad, his brow furrowed. His chicken must be the most fascinating thing he's ever seen because he refuses to look up from it.

"You remember," Mom says. "His new little friend, and that sweet girl he was with."

"He's not my 'little friend,'" I say to Mom, because I'm not five.

"Those kids who left you in the woods?" says Dad, and when he says it like that . . .

"Ted, they didn't *leave him in the woods*, for goodness sake," says Mom.

"Sure seemed like it to me," says Dad, and I can't help but feel relieved that he sounds grumpy and protective instead of all weird and defensive over nothing.

"It must have been pretty interesting," Mya says, bringing us back on topic. "The work," she says when we get quiet.

"Mmhmm," says Dad.

Enlightening. Thanks.

This would all be so much easier if he understood I was just trying to *help* him. Well, okay, and myself and Mya and Mom, too, but seriously, all these secrets are just making it worse. If Dad thinks we're giving him the third degree, just wait until Enzo, intrepid student reporter, shows up on our doorstep.

My stomach curls over my chicken as I imagine the *other* people we've been worried about showing up: men dressed in black coats and hats, banging from the other side of the door, looking for answers about what happened at the parks in Australia or Japan or Maine.

They started asking questions in Germany. We left before they could ask more.

Suddenly, I feel like I might pass out, and it's so hot in here, and I think the chicken might have been bad, and why won't he just talk? Why won't he trust his own family?

"Aaron, are you okay? You look like you're going to be sick," says Mom, reaching for my wrist, and her hand is ice-cold. It feels so good, but I can barely hear her. It's like she's a million miles away.

"Mya, get a wet rag for your brother," says Mom, and Mya stares at me. I stare back. One of us has to do it.

"Mya, do what I said!" says Mom, trying to maintain control, but we're unraveling.

"Why is everything such a secret?" I blurt, and Mya drops her fork onto her plate with a clink.

Mom's hand tightens around my wrist. "Aaron," she hisses, like there's any chance in the world my dad might not have heard.

I stare at the top of Dad's head. I wait for him to look up.

"Why does everyone seem to know something about Grandma and Grandpa?" I say, doing everything I can to keep my voice even. It doesn't work, though. It breaks right in the middle of my sentence, making me sound like I'm pleading. Maybe I am.

Finally, Dad looks up, his head rising slowly. When his eyes are perfectly level with mine, he says, "I really wouldn't know."

Never has such a bland sentence sounded so angry.

Dad holds my eyes until I think they're going to melt in my skull. Then, he slowly sets his fork down, shoves his plate away from him, pushes himself away from the table, and walks calmly down the back hall of the house to his office.

I don't realize I'm shaking until Mya finally gets up and gets me that wet rag. Mom lays it over the top of my head, a little trick she used to employ whenever I had a fever. I have no idea what I have now.

Is there a cure for regret?

I want to take it all back. I thought I was protecting Dad—the whole family, really—but all I've done is upset my mom and scare Mya and make my dad look at me like I'm some kind of curse, all for wondering why our family has to sew secrets up inside of ourselves. At some point, those seams are going to burst, and when they do, it's going to be a mess.

It doesn't matter, though. Dinner is ruined, the night is ruined, and I think maybe my life is ruined, too.

It's so much easier to be sarcastic when you're scared. It's better than the alternative, which I'm pretty sure involves sinking deep into the floor and hiding from the rest of the world.

That night, we all go to bed without saying good night. We take our separate corners, which we have now in this great big house; Dad is right about that. I can still hear everyone, though. I hear Mya brush her teeth and settle into her squeaky bed. I hear Mom sniff and blow her nose about a million times. Her nose runs when she cries. I hear Dad make his way to bed a lot earlier than he normally does. I hope he's checking on Mom.

I wait until all the creaking and nose-blowing and muffled whispers are quiet, and then I wait a long time after that. I'm trying to work up the courage to know what it is I need to do. I keep telling myself it's not for me; it's for Mya. That's not entirely true, though.

Then, as quietly as I can, I lower myself from the top bunk, change into regular clothes, and step lightly into Mya's room. She's flat on her back, arms splayed, nose in the air. She's snoring, and I log it into my memory to tell her about that later.

I nudge her shoulder, which only makes her snort louder at first, so I roll her halfway over until she finally startles awake.

"Why were you snorting in my ear?" she says.

Focus. This isn't the time.

"C'mon, get your jeans on. We're getting some answers."

It only takes her a second to register what I've said, and another to decide she'll do it.

"This had better be good," she grumbles as we sneak out of her room and down the hall.

It isn't. It isn't good at all.

CHAPTER 8

The last thing I want to do is return to these woods. Even worse, to return to them in the middle of the night, equipped with nothing but a couple of flashlights we found in the basement, with my little sister in tow. Everything in me knows this is a horrible idea.

But I'm protecting Mya from absolutely nothing by pretending that everything is hunky-dory. She already has Mom and Dad for that. What she needs—what *we* need—is the truth. If we can find it before the entire town of Raven Brooks does, maybe we can keep the worst of it from coming out.

"The kids in class have told me things about these woods," Mya whispers. The air is so still, I can hear her, even though she's several steps behind me.

"Get up here," I say. "Don't make me have to explain to Mom and Dad how I lost you in the woods in the dead of night."

I really, really don't like the way the word "dead" sounded coming out of my mouth just now.

"Then maybe you should just tell me why we're out here. I swear, you're just like— "

"Don't say it," I warn.

We reach the part of the forest where I got separated from

Enzo and Trinity, and I realize that I have absolutely no idea how to make my way back to the weather station without sliding down the same embankment I rolled down the last time I was here. I can still make out the smooth patch of dirt where my foot slipped.

"What is it?" Mya asks.

"We have to get down there."

"But there's a different way to get down there," she says.

I look at her.

"Because you wouldn't drag me down a hill full of blackberry thorns and poison ivy and who knows what sort of night creatures."

I freeze. *Night creatures.* I was so focused on getting back to the weather station, I somehow managed to forget what it was I was running from last time.

"Forest Protectors," I mumble, and Mya's eyes widen.

"Forest what?"

I shake my head. "It's nothing."

"Well, that makes me feel loads better," she says. "Seriously, if you wanted to creep me out, you didn't need to drag me all the way into the woods to do it."

"Let's just go," I say, grabbing her arm and coaxing her down the hill sideways. I go first so I can kick anything out of the way that we might trip over.

It takes a lot longer to get down the hill when you're not tumbling like a human barrel.

When we reach the clearing, I have to beat back the paranoia that comes from standing in an open space.

"Now where?" whispers Mya. If she's still whispering, then she's feeling it, too. Someone might hear us; someone or some-*thing* hiding in the woods.

I point to the other side of the clearing. "That way."

She gives me one pleading look, then takes off at a sprint, and I don't catch up with her until we reach the other side.

"Way to rip the bandage off," I sputter while she barely struggles to catch her breath. "Through here," I say, picking my way carefully now. This last leg of the journey is a bit of a blur, with me running for my life and all, but I try to blink that memory away because all I'd been hearing was Mr. Gershowitz, right? I keep my eyes open for the tower that seemed to crop up out of nowhere last time.

I'm so focused on the task that I don't even realize that Mya isn't walking beside me anymore. She's a few paces back, still as a statue, staring into the thick darkness to her left.

"What're y—?"

"Shhh!" she warns, holding her hand up. She squints closer into the trees. "Did you hear that?"

"What?" I ask, trying to stay calm, but she's not making it easy.

Mya doesn't answer. Instead, she's still for a second longer, then drops her hand and shakes her head.

"Must have been my imagination," she whispers, and neither of us believes that for a second.

"Come on," I say, hustling her in front of me. "We're almost there."

Please let us be almost there.

We walk the rest of the way in silence, Mya no longer pestering me about where it is I'm dragging her. When we finally arrive at the outbuilding, I watch her look up at the tower the same way I did—like it seems to have no place in this otherwise dense forest.

I wave her toward the corner I rounded the last time, and there's the door, just as I left it, slightly ajar with its lock broken off.

"Is that . . . ?" Mya starts to ask, motioning toward the door.

"Yeah, I might have done that."

"No follow-up questions, right?" she says.

"No follow-up questions."

I take the lead now, edging through the crack in the door, but not without making it creak just enough to send a shiver through me, and once again, I'm staring down the expanse of a long, dark corridor.

At least this time I sort of know where I'm going.

"What is this place?" Mya asks, her voice echoing in a way I don't remember mine doing the last time I was here.

"Mr. Gershowitz says it's a weather station."

"Mr. Gershowitz?" Mya asks.

"Oh yeah. I might have, er, failed to mention the part where he sort of . . . I mean, it was actually kind of funny—"

"He caught you snooping around here after you broke in," says Mya.

"Yep. That's pretty much it."

"You're on your way to becoming a legit criminal."

"Thank you."

"I mean, it's cool and all, Aaron. I'm just not sure why you had to show it to me in the middle of the night. *Tonight* of all nights," she says.

We arrive at our grandparents' old office.

"This is why."

Mya steps into the middle of the room as I find the camping lantern to shed some light. I let Mya look around without saying another word.

Eventually, she arrives at the wedding picture of our grandparents. She picks it up and studies it for some time before setting it down and looking at me, squinting past the lantern light.

"They worked here?"

I nod.

"This was all theirs?"

I shrug. "At least the stuff in this room, I guess."

Mya shakes her head, crinkling her brow while she continues to stare at the shambles of the office.

"Why would this all be such a secret? Why doesn't Dad want to talk about this?"

"This is why you had to see it tonight," I say to Mya. Because this is the night we learned that no matter what, Dad is never going to tell us what our family is hiding, what the rest of Raven Brooks is so eager to know.

Mya continues to poke around, and soon, I'm joining her because I realize my first visit to the weather station got cut short.

Sadly, there's little more to discover now that I have Mya to help me and ample time to sift through what remains. There are old crumbling notebooks dated from 1960–1963, most of them containing words and references and calculations I couldn't begin to understand, even if the ink wasn't already smeared and faded. There are charts drawing lines to latitude lines and axis points, some with the little dents of a compass still present in the paper. There are permits and contracts with signatures and official-looking stamps, and piles of file folders, most of which are either empty or filled with carbon copies of pages too light to read anymore.

Occasionally, there are the more personal artifacts, proof that Roger and Adelle Peterson were real people with real, everyday lives, no matter the genius reputation that seemed to haunt them. There was the Raven Brooks University mug with the school's seal—the large, shadowy wing of a raven encircled by filigree. There are the random newspaper articles folded over to expose the feature written about one of their accomplishments, always picturing one or both of them looking reluctant to stand for a picture. There's even a pearl button from what I imagine came off of one of our grandmother's cardigans.

"Aaron, look at this."

Mya's holding a dusty framed picture I didn't notice the last time I was here, maybe because it was facedown in a corner by the emptied filing cabinet. When I shine the lantern over her shoulder, I see that it's a crude drawing of a clown.

"I could have gone an entire lifetime without seeing that," I say, but Mya shoves me.

"No, dummy, look!"

She points to the more adult-looking script at the bottom reading "Teddy, Age 5."

"Oh."

"Right," she says. "Dad drew this."

We stare at it for a moment in silence, as though we could somehow divine from it the countless memories Dad will never share with us. What could be so bad about this, a boring old weather station with a bunch of moldy papers and abandoned furniture?

"Have you explored the rest of this place yet?" Mya asks.

I shake my head. "Nah, I sort of got, er, sidetracked last time. Why?"

"Don't you think it's weird that it was just . . . abandoned? I mean, why would they leave some of this stuff behind?"

She looks back down at the drawing in her hand, the one that was special enough to frame at one time.

"Maybe they condemned the building or something," I say, but I know that's reaching.

"Then why is it still here?" Mya says, shaking her head. "It seems like they left in a hurry, like they didn't have time to take much."

"Well, whatever the reason," I say, because I can tell she's starting to get scared, "I'm sure it was a good one. Probably not a very exciting one, either."

"Aaron?" she says, and I know she's about to ask me something big. Mya always makes perfect eye contact when she's

Teddy, Age 5

about to ask something big. It makes it impossible for me to lie, which I'm sure she knows.

"Do you think Grandma and Grandpa were like Dad?"

I should have seen the question coming. I don't know if I'm off my game because we moved from Germany so fast or because everything about living in Raven Brooks has been like navigating an obstacle course. Either way, her question takes me off guard, and I don't have time to set my face. She sees my first, unfiltered response before I even say a word.

"The park in Germany," Mya says, and her voice has dropped so low, I can hardly hear her. "It wasn't his fault, was it?"

I have no idea how hard it was for Mya to get that question out, but what I do know for sure is that she was the only one brave enough to ask it.

I open my mouth to answer her, still not sure what I'll say, but instead of words, a high, thin howl is the only thing that comes out.

Mya tilts her head, confused at my response, but the sound didn't come from me.

"You heard that, too?" I say. Because I've heard that noise before.

"It wasn't from in here," she says. "But it was close."

Still holding the framed drawing of a clown, Mya pokes her head out the door, but I pull her back.

"Hang on there, Nancy Drew. Unless you've got some secret ninja skills I don't know about, maybe we shouldn't go hunting for trouble."

"So, what exactly are we doing here tonight?" she challenges.

"Okay, it's possible I didn't think it through all the way," I say, "but I think this is enough excitement for one night."

"What is that sound, though? It almost sounds like a howl, or—"

"All I know is it isn't the first time I've heard it."

"Huh?"

"In the basement at home. And maybe in Dad's study, too. And my room."

". . . huh?"

"Look, I don't know, okay?" I say, getting antsy. "But whether it's the wind or a coyote or Forest Protectors, we're not hanging around to find out."

"Hold on, Forest what?"

"Mya, let's *go!*"

"Okay, okay," she says, shoving me ahead of her. "Just let me gather a few things first. We might never make it back out here again . . . the construction site for the park isn't far. This place could actually get condemned tomorrow."

Reluctantly, I scramble to help her collect a few of our grandparents' notebooks, the maps, and the newspaper articles scattered about the room. We shove them inside a paper bag we find in the desk drawer, then move.

I take a shallow breath and ease myself along the wall toward the door leading back out to the forest. While I'm not excited to return to the rustle of the trees, at least the sound of that weird howling is growing more distant.

"Almost there," I tell Mya before emerging from the door, still ajar, and quickly rounding the corner back to the path that will lead us toward the clearing.

Except when I turn around, Mya's gone.

"Mya, that's not funny," I say, loud enough to let her know I mean it, but the second she doesn't answer, a bottomless hole opens up inside of me, and I feel like I'm falling so fast I'll never get a foothold. My vision goes black for a moment before I get a grip.

"Mya!"

I sprint back toward the open door and jog to the abandoned

office, the lantern still glowing in the middle of the floor where we left it. But Mya is nowhere to be found.

"Where did you . . . Mya?"

My voice reverberates off of the walls and comes crashing back to me, slicing through the thick air of the weather station and bouncing across the crevices I can't see.

I bolt back out the door, my feet pounding on the forest floor as I sprint one length of the wall, then round a corner to the next side.

"MYA!"

I round the third corner, crashing through overgrowth and scraping my knuckles against the thorn bushes, but I can hardly feel a thing.

How could she be gone so fast? It's like she just disappeared.

I round the final corner, and it's the thickest overgrowth yet, vines and gnarled roots weaving a sloppy tapestry across my path.

All at once, I slam straight into something on the other side of the brush, and now my vision does go black, but not from panic. I lie there until the night sky stops spinning and finally crawl to my feet. But not before I see a familiar shoe sticking out from the tangle of shrubs in front of me.

I part the brush and find Mya leaning back on her elbows, trying to regain her own vision.

"Where the heck were you?" I accuse.

"*Me?* Where were *you*? Cute joke abandoning me in there, Jerk!"

"I didn't abandon you! How hard is it to go out the door?"

"I *did* go out the door!"

"Well, clearly you didn't because when I turned around you were gone!"

"So what, you think I found a worm hole?"

Mya's bleeding. It's just a little cut right above her eyebrow, but I can't help but feel like I've failed as a big brother. She's still clutching the paper bag to her chest like it's treasure.

"Come on," I say, making an effort to soften my voice. I lift the bottom of my shirt to her head, and she flinches back.

"Ew, you stink."

"Just hold still."

I dab at her head until the cut is clear, then I help her to her feet and ease her behind me.

"This was a bad idea," I say.

"A little late for that," she grumbles, but she holds tighter to my hand as I guide us through the brush and back to the clearing.

We don't say another word for the rest of the way home, not even when a squirrel skitters up a nearby tree and practically gives us both heart attacks. One of us might have screamed.

When we arrive back at the rambling blue house, Mya and I slowly open the door and sneak back upstairs like thieves. Mya finally releases my hand to slip into the bathroom, dabbing water on the cut above her eye.

I'm in the top bunk when I hear the floor at my doorway creak.

Mya doesn't even ask. She simply hides the paper bag under my bed, lies down on the bottom bunk under me, and pulls the comforter over her head. I'm not sure which of us falls asleep first. All I know is that once we were down, neither of us moved an inch.

CHAPTER 9

Enzo is pacing back and forth behind me so much, I don't even need to watch him to get dizzy.

"Dude, I'm getting motion sickness just *listening* to you."

"It has to be epic. I mean, like nothing she's ever seen."

"It's Halloween, not a meeting with the queen."

How can I be expected to sketch under these conditions?

"And you're sure you have everything you need for yours?" he asks, full of urgency.

"It's not exactly complicated," I say. "Bloody clothes. Butcher knife. Giant Styrofoam tooth."

We've decided to go as the two most notorious, bloodthirsty, infamous slasher movie monsters in the history of ever: me as Smiley, from the always classic *Tooth* series, Enzo as the three-headed alien from *SpaceKills*. We're solid on the idea front; it's the execution that needs a little work.

"Okay, so that leaves me. I need something that can support three heads." He stops pacing for a blissful second. "Hey, have you got a set of shoulder pads? Like from football?"

I look down at my favorite shirt—the one that I've worn for three years and still never managed to adequately fill out.

"Is that a joke?"

Enzo resumes pacing.

"Okay, so no shoulder pads. Maybe I can make something happen with a couple of wire coat hangers. How are those sketches coming?"

"Man, seriously, you have to calm down. I can smell your desperation from over here."

Enzo sighs and slumps on the bottom bunk of my bed. "What if she thinks I'm lame?"

I put my hand on his shoulder and lean in. "Enzo, she already *knows* you're lame—"

"Thanks," he says, throwing my hand off.

"But," I say, "she likes you anyway. Maybe she even thinks you're cool because of it."

"She thinks I'm cool?"

I shrug. How the heck would I know? "Absolutely."

Enzo lightens up enough to actually look at my drawings of the costumes which, if I do say so myself, are amazing.

"These look great," he says.

"I know."

"So, my dad's on this new health kick lately, and the only thing he eats are things that sprouted from other things, so I'm basically starving all the time now," says Enzo. "Please tell me you have an actual potato chip in your kitchen."

"I think there's some leftover pot roast," I say.

"Good enough," he says, getting a head start down the stairs toward the kitchen.

When we reach the bottom of the steps, though, Enzo stops

dead in his tracks. My dad looms over him like a gargoyle, and I wish I could read his expression, but the late afternoon sun is casting a glare on everything above his mustache.

I haven't seen him all day.

"Um," says Enzo.

Nice. Good first impression.

"We were just . . . pot roast . . ." he says after my dad says exactly nothing.

Okay, so maybe there are worse impressions to make.

"Dad, this is my friend Enzo," I say.

I watch his mustache. It doesn't even flinch.

"Pleased to meet you," Enzo says.

My dad is silent. He's like a ghost. I can feel Enzo's nerve melting out of his pores.

"Pleased to meet you . . . *sir?*"

"Enzo," Dad finally says, but he says it so slowly, I'm not sure it's any better than him staying mute. "Enzo Esposito."

"Th-that's right," says Enzo, and I swear he's visibly trembling now.

Either something has taken over my dad's body and is using him as a host, or he's messing with Enzo because he thinks it's funny. Either way, I wish he'd stop.

"We've already met," my dad says.

I can hear Enzo's throat click as he swallows. "Yes, sir. Last m-month."

Great. Yes, let's bring up the night I came home soaked and trembling after Enzo and Trinity lost me in the woods.

"Dad," I say, trying to coax him away from the memory, "It wasn't Enzo's fault. Or Trinity's. I shouldn't have . . ."

I mean, I shouldn't have done a lot of things that day: convinced Enzo and Trinity to take me to the woods, made them tell me about the Forest Protectors, gotten myself so hopelessly lost I had to be chaperoned back to my house like a toddler.

But the shortcut is, "It wasn't their fault."

Dad says nothing.

I take a step down so I'm right behind Enzo, and now that the glare is off his face, I can see Dad's eyes sparkling. It's the kind of shine they get when he's joking. It's also the way they shine when he's angry. At the moment, it's a toss-up.

That is, until he bursts into a laugh so sudden, Enzo and I let out a simultaneous chirp, and he backs into me hard enough to almost knock me off the step.

"I'm pleased to meet you, Enzo," says Dad, his broad smile spreading under his mustache. "Under better circumstances this time."

Dad gives us both a sort of scolding look, but nothing serious. He's just playing.

"In fact, I just heard from your father this afternoon, Enzo," says Dad, and poor Enzo hasn't fully recovered, so I have to ask the follow-up questions.

"Was he looking for Enzo?"

Dad shakes his head casually. "A quote, actually. Or maybe a longer conversation. Something about a story you're working on?" says Dad.

Something in his voice has shifted again. The ease of tone is strained somehow now, like it's an effort to keep his smile pasted on his face. Now it just looks like he's baring his teeth.

"Oh, right," Enzo says, his voice barely above a whisper. "My story."

"A young reporter, are you?" Dad asks Enzo.

"N-no. I mean, no, sir. I mean, not yet. Maybe."

Dad laughs another of his booming laughs, and the sound of it echoes off the stairway. "Well, so long as you're decisive."

Enzo looks to me to make sure it's okay to laugh along with my dad before he eventually lets his shoulders fall.

"I think it could be a really interesting story," says Enzo, and now it's time for *my* shoulders to tense up.

"Well," says my dad with practiced modesty, "I don't want to disappoint you, young man, but we aren't exactly the Kennedys. Don't expect too much excitement."

"Are you kidding? A world-famous theme park designer? Top secret scientists? Most people's parents are, well, I don't know what most people's parents do. But you're more interesting than that," says Enzo, somehow managing to be totally inappropriate and charming all at the same time.

Dad gives Enzo a warm smile, and that should make me feel better; he's not mad. But Enzo's mention of the theme park twists my stomach up so tight, I think I might toss my tacos from lunch.

"Did you boys say something about getting some food?" asks Dad, suddenly Mr. Hospitality.

"Actually, I'm feeling a little sick," I say, totally underselling it because I'm fairly certain I'm going to puke all over these stairs in a moment.

171

Enzo shrugs. "I've gotta get home anyway. Dad's weird about homework."

I couldn't be more relieved that Mr. Esposito is weird about anything.

The minute Enzo pulls the front door closed, I spin on the step and try to make my way to the upstairs bathroom, but Dad's hand is around my wrist before I can get very far.

"Did you tell his father to call me?" Dad asks. I look for the same gleam in his eyes that was there a second ago when Enzo was standing beside me. The spark is gone; his eyes have turned a dull, flat green.

"No, of course not," I say, feeling caught, even though I've done nothing wrong.

Dad searches me with his empty eyes, and I try so hard to divine what it is he's looking for. A lie? A way to blame me? A way to take back the accusation I didn't earn?

The grip on my arm loosens, and I'm allowed to slowly pull away.

If he was looking for a lie, he won't find it. I've done nothing but try to keep trouble away. If he's looking for a way to blame me, I wish he'd do it already instead of constantly searching. If he's looking for a way to take it all back, it's too late. I already heard the distrust in his voice. He doesn't trust me with our secrets, but he still expects me to guard them.

I can feel his eyes on me as I make my way up the stairs and down the hall to my room. I don't feel like I'm going to throw up anymore. Instead, I climb into bed and curl myself into a ball on my side, waiting for the sky to turn gray, then black, pretending not to hear when Mom calls me for dinner, pretending to sleep when Mya creeps in to say good night.

At some point, pretending to sleep turns into real sleep, and I only realize I've dozed when Mya's screams wake me up.

I'm down the bunk and onto the floor in less than a second, hurrying into her room before she can wake Mom and Dad. It's one of her nightmares again.

"Mya, shhhhh," I try soothing her, and to my surprise, she responds. Or it seems like it until I realize she's talking in her sleep.

She's mumbling at first, but when I lean closer, I hear her clearly.

"They can't breathe. Someone, help, they can't breathe!"

I draw back on my heels. All the warmth leaves my body as I try to erase Mya's sleeping pleas, but they're words I can't forget. They're words I'll *never* forget.

The sound of rushing water fills my ears, and all at once, I'm back there.

Fernweh Welt is electric with chaos.

Crowds surge like waves, and Mya and I are fighting upstream, up the ramps and up the stairs to the top platform, past the lines of tired and curious patrons, their curiosity turning to wonder, to suspicion, to fear as we climb higher.

"Something's gone wrong," they say.

Mya's hand grips mine as I pull her, weaving through bodies and slipping on water. Then from behind, a bigger hand holds mine, a slim one with bony fingers and a comforting softness.

"It's okay," Mom tells us, breathless from racing to catch up. She's still in her performance costume. She's still in her dance

shoes. The water dripping from the ramps above settles into the
soft suede. The hem of her delicate dress is smeared with dirt.

The hem of her dress is what I'm staring at when the woman's
scream from above slices through the air, tilting every head
in line.

Under the gasps of the people, I pull my mom closer.

"It's not okay," I tell her, and she closes her eyes.

When I open my eyes, I'm sitting on the floor beside Mya's bed. Her eyes are still again, her forehead smooth.

I have no idea where Mya goes when the nightmares stop, but wherever it is, I wish she'd take me with her. I'd give anything to be there, too.

I go back to my room, steeped in its midnight darkness. I'm so tired, but there's no doubt in my mind that I'll be awake for the rest of the night. I'll get to see the nighttime give way to daylight, and I'll tell myself over and over again that it wasn't okay in Germany, but maybe there's still a chance that it will be okay in Raven Brooks. If I can keep all the intrusive questions and prying eyes at bay, maybe I can give us a fighting chance at a normal life here.

In a night this bleak, that's the most hope I can muster.

CHAPTER 10

Halloween on a weekday feels like an unreasonable compromise for a kid to have to make.

Yes, children, you may wear your costumes to school, but no, you may not enjoy it. Yes, you may eat ten pounds of candy, but you may not behave energetically afterward. Yes, you may wear costume makeup, but no fake blood, excessive glitter, sprayed hair, or dangling eyes, ears, or other body parts. No tripping or slipping hazards, no props.

No fun.

By the time we've finished out the school day, our Halloween excitement has waned. Trinity—a comic book supervillain of her own creation—looks far less intimidating now that she knows there'll be an algebra test at the end of the week. Mya, a rabid bunny, looks more or less like a regular bunny thanks to the no fake blood rule. Maritza, thematically the best costume of the bunch as a Golden Apple mystery candy, is less mysterious now that this year's candy has finally been revealed as perhaps the world's biggest letdown: peppermint. But she'd already made the costume, handstitched and painted, and it was too late to turn back. Enzo couldn't wear the shoulder pads with his additional two heads after we determined he wouldn't fit through any classroom door, so he didn't bother wearing his costume to school at all. Ditto for me; without the fake blood, Smiley might just look like a deranged beaver.

"Halloween's a bust," pouts Mya. "We should just skip it this year."

"What? No way. That's what they *want* you to do," says Enzo, reliably optimistic as ever.

"Who's 'they'?" asks Mya.

Enzo struggles. "You know . . . the Man. The ones who make the rules."

Mya blinks at him.

"We have to go trick-or-treating," says Trinity. "We haven't gotten to see Enzo's costume yet."

It might be my imagination, but I'd swear I just saw Enzo start to glow.

"Or Aaron's," she adds diplomatically, and Enzo's shine fades a little.

"Besides, what about all those peppermint Golden Apples we'd miss out on?" I say, and Maritza gets mad all over again.

"Of all the flavors," she rants, for at least the fourth time this week. "How could they mess it up that badly? *Peppermint?* Why not just call it what it is: Chocolate Toothpaste!"

Trinity puts a sympathetic hand on her shoulder. "You'll get through this difficult time."

"Seven o'clock at the end of our street," says Enzo. "We'll meet up there and devise a plan."

We all agree, then Trinity makes her way to the bus pickup while the rest of us walk home.

"It'll be better once we can all amp up our costumes again," I reassure Mya, and she seems to perk up when I tell her she can use some of my fake blood.

When we get home, that enthusiasm fades.

No one is speaking when we walk through the door, but the air is dense with what's already been spoken. Or shouted, or cried. Whatever it was, Mom is now in the kitchen aggressively chopping mushrooms for dinner and Dad is in his study moodily ruminating over his designs.

"Did everyone like your costume, sweetheart?" Mom asks Mya, her happiness so forced it's like she's pushing it through her teeth when she smiles.

Mya nods. It's not worth telling Mom it was actually lame.

"Do you have everything ready for yours tonight?" Mom asks me.

"Yup. Just need to add some finishing touches," I say.

Mom starts chopping faster, her knife grinding hard against the cutting board, and I wonder what it is I've said.

"Just like your father." She laughs, but not really. Her voice is weirdly high. "Never quite done. Never quite good enough."

"I didn't mean—"

"Oh, I know you didn't, darling," she says, marking maybe the first time ever that she's called me "darling." She's acting like Mya and I are guests she has to entertain.

"Mom, can we, um, help you or anything?" Mya asks, and I'm not sure she means with dinner.

"Just go on up to your room and finish your homework, kids," she says, sounding a tiny bit more like herself but still not looking up. "No homework, no Halloween."

It isn't until dinnertime that we return to the land of the non-fighting parents, where everything they say to each other is a not-so-subtle dig, and every question about why they're fighting is answered with "We're not fighting; what makes you think we're fighting?"

"These mushrooms are interesting," says Dad, peering at a spoonful swimming in gravy on his spoon.

"I'm not sure what that's supposed to mean, but okay," says Mom, pressing her teeth together again.

Dad lets the mushroom fall from his spoon and splat back into his bowl before raising his eyes to Mom.

"Have you always put mushrooms in the beef stew?"

"Have you always had so much interest in mushrooms?" Mom shoots back.

Game on. It appears they're tied at the moment.

Dad takes a bite and grimaces. Mom watches him and slurps her next spoonful with gusto.

"We're meeting everyone at seven," I say, wading into the conversation. This is my only chance to get an extension on our normal curfew.

"That's great, hon," says Mom, even though it's not great. It's not anything, really.

"And we have a lot of ground to cover," adds Mya.

"Of course," says Dad, about as engaged as Mom is, which is to say we could be talking about circus bears right now and they wouldn't know it. This could work out well, actually.

"And we were thinking that if we had a little more time, we'd be able to hit another neighborhood. Which would just mean a tiny extension of our curfew to nine, and—"

"No," says Dad.

"But if we—"

"No."

"Dad," Mya tries, "I'll be with Aaron, and Trinity is almost twelve, so—"

"Your father said 'no,'" says Mom, and on this and this alone, Mom and Dad seem to be aligned.

"But why not?" I whine.

"There's going to be a storm tonight," Dad says.

HOMEWORK IS BORING AND I HATE DOING IT.

1.)
$$2a + 7 = 19$$
$$-7 \quad -7$$
$$2a + 0 = 12$$
$$2a = 12$$
$$a = 6$$

2.)
$$6a + 4 = 34$$
$$-4 \quad -4$$
$$6a + 0 = 30$$
$$6a = 30$$
$$a = 5$$

I look outside at the clear skies illuminated by the setting sun.

"I don't remember the news saying anything about that," I say, tempting fate by challenging Dad, but I think I can recognize an excuse when I hear it.

I immediately regret my bravery when he trains his eyes on me.

"You have no idea how severe they can get in this area," he says. "What you saw the other night? That was nothing."

I've never heard him—heard anyone, really—talk about weather like it's a boogeyman.

"Okay," I say, backing away from the argument with both hands up in surrender. "Got it. We'll be home before the storm."

Dad burns a hole through my head while he stares me in the

eyes, the seriousness of his warning completely lost on me. What isn't lost on me, though, is how much he doesn't look like my dad. Right in this moment, he doesn't even look like someone I recognize. That to me is way scarier than any storm.

"Were the storms bad when you were growing up?" Mya asks Dad. "Were you afraid of them?"

Dad stiffens. "No."

"You seem tense," Mom says, sounding pretty tense herself. "Why don't you call up Ike and see if he wants to grab a coffee. It's been a while since you've gotten out."

"I didn't realize I was being monitored," says Dad.

Back away, Mom.

But she doesn't. "It's not 'monitoring' you if I'm worried about you," she says pointedly.

There's something brewing in Dad's belly now. I can tell. And it doesn't have anything to do with the beef stew.

"Perhaps we can talk about your concerns when we're not sitting at the dinner table as a family," Dad grinds out.

Translation: not in front of the kids, which is a joke considering their fight could be seen from space.

"What's wrong with suggesting you spend some time with an old friend?" Mom asks because she's the only one in this house brave enough to push it this far.

Just then, I remember someone else who pushed Dad recently: the very same Ike Gershowitz Mom is talking about.

"Well, thank you for your concern, dear," says Dad coldly, "but Ike hasn't seen fit to call me back after our disagreement."

"Oh," says Mom, only embarrassed for a second before she looks worried. "I didn't realize you'd fought."

The knot in my stomach draws tighter as I remember that night, the way Dad had turned so icy toward his oldest friend, just like he's doing with Mom now. It's like he's building this wall around himself, and unless he builds a door, pretty soon it's going to be impossible to reach him.

"There's a lot you don't realize," says Dad.

"I think I'm full," I say, and Mya rests her spoon in her bowl, too.

"May we be excused?" she asks, and Mom just nods. She and Dad are locked in a staring contest. I can't leave the table fast enough.

When we leave for trick-or-treating—bunny ears and giant tooth and fake blood in place—Mom and Dad have only six parting words for us:

"Have fun. Be safe. Eight thirty."

Mya and I nod silently and walk out of the house, the air outside a relief from whatever that was in our house.

I wait for Mya to say something, but she seems too deep in her own thoughts, and I can't help but be glad because I have no idea what I'd say to her anyway.

Trick-or-treaters are already knocking on doors and darting down the street by the time we meet up with the rest of the gang.

Enzo looks amazing. I don't know where he found the football pads, but they hold the papier-mâché heads up perfectly. It's nearly identical to my sketch, and I'm not sure I've ever felt prouder. Lucy Yi has joined Maritza, too, and Mya greets her with a hug and a little squeal because Lucy is a T. rex, and a pretty impressive one at that.

"My mom painted the scales herself," says Lucy, and I take note of the iridescent skin on the back of her stitched spine all the way to her long tail.

"Okay, it's plan time," says Trinity, getting right down to work.

"I have some critical data to share," says Enzo, and we're all ears.

He leans in a little closer, dropping his voice. "Okay, nobody react. We don't want to draw attention. But I have it on good authority that Delwood Heights is handing out FULL-SIZED CANDYBARS."

Maritza gasps.

"Shhhh," Enzo warns, covering her mouth with his hand. "Be cool!"

"Sorry, it's just—"

"They say that every year. It's never true," says Trinity.

Enzo shakes his head slowly, his eyes deadly serious. "Not this time. My source actually witnessed the purchase of said candy. In bulk."

Lucy screws up her face, which is barely visible inside the wide mouth of the dinosaur head. "Who is this source of yours?"

Enzo guffaws. "I can't reveal that! It's code!"

"What code?"

"It's . . . candy code. Or Halloween code. I don't know, but it's not allowed."

"How do we know it's trustworthy intel?" asks Trinity.

"It is," says Enzo. "Frankly, I'm beginning to take it a little personally that you're all so ready to doubt me."

"We believe you," I say, putting a hand on one of Enzo's heads. "It's just that Mya and I have to be back by eight thirty."

Enzo's quiet while he thinks it through. His own face creases in concentration while the two on his shoulders stare blankly into the night.

Then, inspiration strikes. "The woods," he says.

"Nope," says Trinity. "No way."

"Wait, you're not saying we—" I start, but no, that can't be.

"Cut through the woods. It's the only way."

"Enzo's right," says Maritza. "Delwood Heights is just over the train tracks. There's no way we'll make it if we use the roads, but it's a straight shot past the factory."

"Have we all forgotten what happened that last time we decided to go trouncing through the woods?" says Trinity.

Mya takes an almost imperceptible step closer to me.

"What about the Forest Protectors?" Lucy says, her voice so tiny inside her fearsome T. rex head, I can barely hear her.

"There's no such thing as Forest Protectors," says Trinity, and boy do I wish I believe that.

"But you know what does exist?" says Enzo. "Candy. Full-sized, no-fooling, chocolate-covered deliciousness. It's real, you guys."

We're all quiet as the gravity of Enzo's words sink in. The thought of everyone else snagging the prized treats—getting more than their share because we were too chicken to cut through the woods—is unbearable. "We're in," I say.

"We are?" says Mya.

I nod.

Trinity sighs. "Okay, but everybody sticks together, got it? No repeats of last time."

We all agree because Trinity is really the only one among us with the authority to demand that level of obedience.

We make our way to the alley as inconspicuously as a group of murderers, carnivores, and human-sized candies are able to. I briefly consider telling them there's an easier way into the forest, but I don't exactly remember how to get there, and besides, if we're trying not to get caught, probably best to avoid the place where I know Mr. Gershowitz sometimes patrols.

Enzo, Maritza, and Lucy all have to remove half of their costumes and pass them through the opening in the fence in order to fit, but eventually, we all make it through.

"This had better be worth it," Maritza grumbles as she reaffixes her wrapper headgear.

"Eyes on the prize, little sis," says Enzo, and Maritza grumbles something under her breath that sounds vaguely like a curse.

We pick our way slowly through the foliage, grateful for the light of a fuller moon this time.

"Hang on, I'm stuck," says Lucy from somewhere behind us. "Can someone untangle me?"

"Just pull the vine," says Trinity.

"I can't reach," Lucy says, waving her tiny dinosaur arms in front of her.

We end up freeing Lucy from shrubs at least three more times, and after Mya swears her leg is starting to itch with poison ivy and one of Enzo's heads falls off and rolls down the same embankment I rolled down, we have all thoroughly had it.

"My eyes aren't on the prize," Maritza says, kicking through dead leaves and dragging her empty candy bag on the ground. "I've forgotten what the prize is."

"How can you forget?" asks Enzo. "You're dressed as the prize."

Maritza scowls. "You promised chocolate. So help me, if we reach Delwood Heights, and all they have are full-sized Peppermint Golden Apples, I swear I'll—"

"I think I see the roof of the factory," says Trinity, and she may be dressed like a villain, but in this moment she's a superhero because the factory means we're close to the other side of the woods. All that stands between us and full-sized goodness after that is a set of train tracks.

We keep walking, and I tell myself every time I hear a twig snap that it was one of us. It definitely wasn't somewhere in the distance, in one of the hundred spots of dark nothingness that surrounds us. It definitely wasn't someone, or something, with talon feet and a bloodthirsty beak following us at a distance.

"Whoa," Trinity says, seeing what we can't see yet up ahead.

When we arrive by her side, we repeat her response, because let's face it, there isn't much else to say.

There, right in the middle of the woods that feel like they could swallow us whole and no one would ever find us, is a swathe of land so barren and bald, it looks like a mistake.

Not even a stump remains where there should be hundreds, and all trace of brush and bush has been scooped, rooted, leveled, and smoothed in preparation for what comes next. Farther back than anyone can see, the land that used to be forest waits to be something else.

According to the sign hanging on a chain-link fence so high no one would dare climb it, the land is waiting to become the Golden Apple Amusement Park. And our dad is waiting to become the name behind the next legendary theme park.

"Kinda weird that this is all going to be roller coasters and rides pretty soon," says Enzo.

My stomach.

"How soon?" I ask.

"I dunno. They said on the tour. Next year I think?"

I hear Mya let out a tiny gasp.

"That's not even possible!" I say, only realizing how defensive I sound after Enzo looks confused.

"Hey, man, that just means that pretty soon, we won't have to drive three hours to Spree Land to scream our heads off. Hey, didn't your dad design a couple of the rides there, too?"

I'm barely listening to Enzo. I'm trying to remember how long it took for Dad to design Fernweh Welt. Eighteen months? Two years? And even then, there were . . . mistakes.

Sure they got together the backing and started clearing the ground a couple of years ago, but all the planning, the construction . . . How is Dad possibly going to finish the designs and the engineering for the Golden Apple Amusement Park in under a year?

"My dad says your dad must be working around the clock to

get everything ready for the ceremony," says Enzo, and suddenly he comes back into focus.

"What ceremony?"

"Dude, how do I know all this stuff and you don't? Don't you live with the guy?"

Be calm. I just need to be calm.

It won't be like before. It won't be.

"The unveiling thing-a-majig," says Enzo, turning to Trinity for help.

"Don't look at me," she shrugs. "You're the town crier."

Enzo looks mortally wounded. "I'm not the—anyway," he

says, turning back to me. "Some of the City Council people want to look important, so they're gonna have a big ceremony."

This night just keeps getting better.

"I told you your family is famous," says Enzo, and I hate so much that he's right.

"Why? Who's your family?" asks Lucy from somewhere inside her suit.

"Roger and Adelle Peterson were his grandparents," says Maritza.

"Wait, you mean the people who burned down the—?"

Enzo and Maritza jump in to stop her, but Trinity is the first one to act, pinching the opening of her T. rex mouth shut.

"Don't do that! It's dark in here!" she says, sounding like she's at the bottom of a hole. But I'm less concerned about the conditions of her suit and more interested in what Lucy was about to say about my grandparents.

"Burned down what?" I say.

"Nothing, it's nothing," says Enzo so unconvincingly, I'm actually a little disappointed in him.

"Look," says Mya, sounding about twenty years older than she is, "whatever it is, I'm sure it can't be that bad, so you might as well just tell us."

"They burned down the first Golden Apple factory," blurts Maritza. "Or I mean, that's what people say. *Some* people. Hardly any people."

"Okay, so maybe it *can* be that bad," says Mya, looking stricken. Her eyes are round and panicky, and she looks even more deranged under all her fake blood and bunny fur.

"That's ridiculous," I say. "I mean, that's ridiculous, right? Who would believe that?"

I start to laugh, hoping the rest of them will join in, but when nobody does, I understand just how many people would believe that.

"Why?" I ask. Maybe I demand. "Why would they do something that . . . ?"

"Illegal?" says Trinity.

"Reckless?" Enzo says.

"Dangerous?" says Maritza.

"Can you please open my mouth?" says Lucy, and Trinity looks confused for a second, then quickly unpinches the dinosaur's face.

"Sorry."

"Pointless," I finish. "I was going to say pointless."

"I guess if you believe the rumors," says Enzo, "it's because the Tavishes stopped giving them money for their research."

"Why would that make them burn down the factory?" says Mya. "What would that have to do with making candy?"

Trinity shakes her head. "Nothing. It was about—"

"Anger," I say, and everyone gets quiet because they know I'm right. "They were mad. So they took it out on the Golden Apple Corporation." I look up. "Because it was the Tavishes' company."

Trinity surprises me by putting a hand gently on my shoulder and finding my gaze, which is no easy task.

"They investigated. A gas line broke. The whole arson thing was just a rumor."

I try to keep her gaze, but as I stare out at the clearing made for the Golden Apple Amusement Park and the horizon beyond it, I catch sight of another familiar silhouette: the tower of the abandoned weather station where my grandparents used to work.

I think back to the article framed in the History Room at the factory, the witnesses who saw two shadowy figures fleeing the scene.

"They were close enough to the factory. What if . . . I mean, it's possible they could have—"

Trinity shakes her head. "Nobody even knows who those supposed witnesses were," she says, seeming to read my mind. "And besides, the fire started in the basement. Security records show no one entered or left the basement that day. There were no signs of forced entry, either. Unless your grandparents figured out how to teleport into the basement of the factory, they didn't set that fire."

I want to feel better. I really do. It's just that the knot in my stomach has found such a nice home, and I don't see it unraveling anytime soon.

"But what if, I don't know, they found a different way in? Like what if there's a sewer system or something?"

"Okay, first of all, gross," says Trinity. "I'm not sure any kind of revenge is worth crawling around in a sewer."

"She has a point," Maritza pipes in.

"Second of all," Trinity continues, "People were so ready to blame your grandparents, the police searched. Trust me, there was no other way for them to get into the factory. They were innocent."

Trinity's explanation should be more than enough to convince me. It also should have convinced everyone else thirty years ago. So why didn't it? Why was everyone so determined to pin the fire on my grandparents?

I also can't shake the realization that even though he knew about these rumors, Enzo still wants to do this stupid story on my family. It's like he can't understand that this isn't just a fun story to share with your buddies when you're trying to freak each other out. These aren't random strangers anymore. These people are my family.

"Did anyone else just feel that?" asks Trinity.

I didn't even realize she'd walked away. Now she's standing in the middle of the path ahead. Her dark green costume should be iridescent under the moonlight. It was before. Now, it's a cloudy, dull gray, and when she tips her head to the sky, she quickly flinches away.

A single *tap* lands somewhere on the leaves above us, then another, then another.

It doesn't take long for the drops to multiply, and in no time, the bright moonlight that had been lighting our path up to this point disappears behind a smear of thick black clouds.

Before we even have a chance to react, the forest begins to flood.

In no time, the dead leaves and pine needles and loose dirt turn to a muddy river under our feet. Wind takes hold of the branches and thrashes them around wildly, and with the wind comes the thunder and lightning, so much worse than the last time that I wonder if this is more than a storm.

This feels violent.

"Come on!" I hear someone scream, but it's impossible to tell who it is.

We should run, but where? Which way?

I thought I'd turned in the opposite direction, but it doesn't look right anymore. The entire landscape of the forest is changed, and soon, the wind is blowing so much rain in my face, it hurts to keep my eyes open.

I drop to a crouch for a second, covering my head with my hands as the torrents fall, and this time when the thunder rumbles, I swear it shakes the ground.

"Mya, stay with me!" I holler into the howling wind, but I don't hear her respond.

I stand from my crouch, shoulders still hunched, and search behind me, but I'm confused to find no one there. I turn to the side, and still no one. I spin faster to the opposite side, beating back the panic that's sneaking in fast, and I find myself alone.

"Where are you guys?!" I yell, loud enough to make my throat catch. Water hits my face so hard it feels like pebbles. Wind swipes at the branch beside me, and it slaps my face with enough force to sting.

"MYA!" I shout, my voice cracking under the strain. I think I hear someone calling back, but the wind is distorting all sound, and whether she's behind me or in front of me or anywhere at all is impossible to say.

When I look up again, the sky isn't blue or gray or black anymore. It's a deep purple, and it's moving.

No, that isn't the sky—it's birds. Hundreds and hundreds of black birds screeching through the sky, not a flock but a swarm, their wings beating in unison with the wind.

"MYA!!"

I begin to run. I don't know if it's the best way or the worst way, but it's all I can do. If I stand still for too long, I might get swept away.

"MYA!"

She could be anywhere. Absolutely anywhere. She was so close to me, and just like that, she wasn't.

A bolt of lightning cracks across the sky, and I know I must be imagining it, but it feels so close, I'd swear I smell burning. The thunder is like an ancient curse, roaring through the sky, seeking vengeance.

I search desperately for something familiar: a tree, a roofline, a path. But the rain is blowing sideways as one solid sheet, and water is filling my ear. Even if she called out for me now, would I be able to hear her?

I stumble over an exposed root and fall to my knees, the shed needles flowing through the stream of rain and pricking my legs and hands. I try to take a breath deep enough, but all I do is sputter.

"Where are you?" I scream.

Where are any of you?

I run and I run, but none of it feels like progress. I try to squint through the storm, but it's like the storm doesn't want me to see.

"It's okay," I yell into the rain, just for myself. "It's okay."

It's okay.

But it's not okay.

Mom told me to stay calm, so that's what I told Mya, and together, holding hands and linked like a chain, we wove in and out of the crowd lining the ramp up to the flume ride. The ramp grew steeper the higher we climbed, but somehow, we managed to run faster.

When we reached the top, we stopped because everyone else was stopped. Compared to the chaos below, the platform observed a strange silence. The ride was frozen, its emergency break thrown, its red lights flashing. The water below rushed, and the sound of it echoed under the dome of the platform, something akin to static. Over the static were the gentle whimpers and whispers of three dripping parkgoers, some with jackets thrown over their shoulders, some leaning on paramedics. Every one of them stared down at the steep drop below, where one of the carts was visibly trapped underwater. The catch designed to pull the carts to the top of the hill had never released, dragging four people under the water for who knows how long.

A ways off from the other three passengers, a man lay on the ground with a paramedic over him. The crouched medic had his back to us, quietly counting as he rocked forward with quick movements. A pair of soaking wet gray tennis shoes pointed to the dome overhead. The body they were attached to lay prone on the ground beside the ride.

Mom squeezed my hand hard, and at some point, I lost

feeling in my fingertips. I squeezed Mya's hand, but I tried not to hold hers so hard.

"His seat belt wouldn't release," someone whispered.

"Someone had to go in and cut it, but by then—"

"He couldn't breathe in the water, so—"

I can't feel my fingers. Or my arms. I think all of me is numb. The man continues to count and press, count and press.

"And he's here with his family."

"I just don't understand how—"

"Something with the chain that pulls the carts—"

"It just didn't let go when they got to the top—"

"Can you even imagine . . . ?"

I try to read Mom's face, but she's turned toward the man on the ground. I want to ask her where Dad is. I want to know why the ride failed.

I want to know if this is why Dad told Mom to keep Mya and me away from the flume.

But Dad isn't anywhere to be found. It's just Mom and Mya and me, the three of us with linked hands and linked guilt because we know something more than the rest of the people here; we knew that the park was built fast, and Dad wasn't happy about that. We knew that for the last week, Dad hadn't been around so much.

Later, we would know that people were looking for him, that there were questions to answer, that Mya and I were allowed to pack three boxes apiece before we left the rest behind.

In those slow-motion minutes on the platform of the flume

ride—by the frozen boats and the water sloshing over the tracks—we stared at the man who pressed on the other man's chest. I watched the unconscious man's shoes point motionless to the sky. At some point, I let go of Mya's hand, and Mom let go of mine, and the man performing compressions stopped, and we all stared at his still body while the prone man's family draped themselves over him.

Then they screamed a single, collective cry.

At first, I think it's a tree trunk I've run into. I'm stunned backward, and I still hear the ringing of screams in my ears. When I finally open my eyes, I'm staring at the dark, starless sky. Clouds still hang low and heavy, the storm not yet through with us, but most of the rain has stopped. The birds, if there ever were any, are gone.

It was my dad—that's what I ran into.

"You have no idea how much trouble you're in," he says so quietly, I can barely hear him over the echoes still cluttering my head. I hear enough, though.

Mom's arms are around me too tightly, and between Mya and her, I don't know who's pressing harder. All I know is that I'm on my feet fast, and it isn't long before I see a band of soggy friends, costumes torn and soaked and dragging, hair wet and eyes big as saucers. Enzo and Maritza have towels around them like capes; supervillain Trinity is covered by her dad's rain jacket.

All the parents have the same look:

We're so relieved you're safe. Now you will die.

"Are you okay?" whispers Enzo, and I only have time to nod before Dad pulls Mya and me away.

"Home. Now."

The walk home was still blustery enough that the silence from my parents wasn't as noticeable. We had the rattling of leaves and the growl of thunder to fill in the spaces. As soon as we close the front door behind us, though, it's just us and the sound of drops hitting the floor under our feet.

"I won't even ask what you were thinking," Mom admonishes as she helps us pull our drenched costumes off and piles them in a heap by the door. "I don't even want to know."

Her voice is shaking. I've heard her voice shake like that before.

When we're free of our Halloween gear, candyless and fearing the imminent wrath of Dad, he finally turns to face us, the dark hallway shadowing his face so we can only see the gleam of his gritted teeth.

"You'll be lucky if you ever get to leave this house again," he says, and he's unnervingly calm. There's no menace in his voice, no quiver like Mom's or quiet fury like Trinity's dad or Mr. Esposito's wordless scolding he managed to do all with his eyes.

Instead, Dad's voice is matter-of-fact, and I've never been more frightened of him than I am in this moment.

"To your rooms," Mom says, and Mya and I drag ourselves up the steps, hearing Dad's study door click shut as we reach the landing. Not even a crack of light leaks from underneath the door.

That night, I hear Mya's door creak open first, followed by some murmuring, a tiny sob, some more murmuring. The storm has all but cleared by now, and my room feels damp and dark with the memory of it. I have no idea what time it is, but it feels late.

When Mya's door shuts, it's mine that opens next. In walks Mom, and to my surprise, she climbs the three-rung ladder on the side of my bunk to lie down beside me.

Even more surprising is when I start to cry. It's not like a full-fledged sobfest or anything; it's just that the knot that usually hangs out in my stomachs seems to have moved up to my throat, and it hurts when I swallow.

She wipes my face dry with the edge of her sleeve and pushes the hair off my forehead. After a minute, I stop crying, and she just keeps pushing my hair back and saying, "It's okay. It's okay."

Is it?

It's not the first time I've wondered how much Mom really knows. Does she know exactly what happened that day at the flume ride? Does she know what it was those people in the dark suits wanted to talk to Dad about afterward? Does she know why we had to leave at night? Does Mom know about the weather station, about the fire at the first factory?

Does she even know who the Petersons are?

These aren't questions I've figured out how to ask. Maybe I'm not asking the right way. Maybe I just don't want to know the answers. I wonder if Mom's the same.

"It's okay," she whispers over and over.

Just like she said to me that night after the flume ride and the man in the sneakers and the family that screamed.

And that night, when I whispered to her: "Was it an accident?" she'd said nothing at all. She just held me tighter.

Just like she's holding me tonight.

CHAPTER 11

It could have been a life sentence for Mya and me. It probably should have been. But after two weekdays of quarantine, the mere presence of us seems to be stressing Dad out.

Apparently, Enzo was right about the Unveiling Ceremony for the Golden Apple Amusement Park. It's going to be a huge deal, and Dad seems to be feeling the pressure in a big way.

"Read a book," he'd growl, or "Go do your homework!"

But we've read all the good books, and we did all our homework. The days after Halloween had at least gotten us out of the house for school, but then came the weekend. By Saturday afternoon, Dad is freaked out enough about his deadline to notice us breathing too loudly.

"I'm going to my study—*again*!" he barks before my mom finally finds her opening.

"Hon, don't you think it would do us all a bit of good to let them get some fresh air?" Mom asks gently, and to my surprise, Dad relents. He really must be at his wit's end.

"But no having fun," he grumbles, and Mya and I have our shoes on faster than Mom can tell us to be home before dinner.

"Air!" Mya cries, tipping her nose to the sky and inhaling deeply. "Glorious air!"

"I thought I'd never see the sun again," I say, and I swear my body actually feels lighter.

"How long until he doesn't want to feed us to a pack of angry sharks?" Mya asks.

"No longer than a year," I say. "Eighteen months maybe."

"I know I should feel bad about all the rest of it, but honestly, it's the candy that bums me out the most."

I nod. It's only like the millionth time it's crossed my mind . . . We got grounded for life, and we didn't get the goods. Not even a Peppermint Golden Apple. Oh, and the full-sized candy bars in Delwood Heights? Real. Seth Jenkins confirmed it, then rubbed our noses in it at lunch on Thursday. I barely know him, and I've never hated him more.

"Trinity's parents made her write a report on the origins of Raven Brooks," says Mya, kicking a pebble out of her way. "Lucy's parents are still deciding on her punishment, so you *know* it's gonna be bad."

I bat away a low-hanging tree branch. "Enzo said he and Maritza had to help out at the *Banner*."

"I'd take that over house arrest any day," says Mya. "And speaking of which . . ."

She produces the bag full of papers we found at the weather station from her backpack.

"I still don't know why you took those," I begin. "We can't understand any of that without a PhD."

"You don't need a PhD to read the newspaper though. And we grabbed at least ten of them."

In the backyard, far from Mom and Dad's eyes, we spread the

articles out and start reading. The first few are just mentions about the research—prizes and grants our grandparents won. But then we come across something a little juicier.

I read the first few sentences of the article:

For local meteorologists and husband-and-wife team Roger and Adelle Peterson, the storm hasn't passed. According to this dynamic duo, their research into the unique weather conditions that have plagued the town of Raven Brooks for as far back as residents can remember is not nearly finished. Despite the devastating and unexpected loss of research funding from the Tavish Society, the Petersons are determined to get to the bottom of the unique and often dangerous weather phenomena that blow through our fair city.

All right, not great, but not unexpected, either. I already knew all this. I pass the article off to Mya, who skims it quickly.

"Why do you think the Tavishes cut their funding?" she asks. "Do you think they discovered something that the Tavishes didn't like?"

"What would they find out? That the storms are bad for tourism?" I say. "I don't think that's enough of a reason to pull their money."

"I don't know. All I know is that Maritza's always telling me how the town gets hit with these crazy storms or flash floods or whatever, but somehow none of the neighboring towns ever have the same thing happen."

I know there's a bigger story here. I can feel us dancing all around it but never quite getting there.

"How did the Tavishes make their money anyway?" I ask.

"It was the Golden Apples, right?"

I shake my head. "The Golden Apples just made them *richer.* They only had the money to buy out Gammy Flo's candy because they were wealthy from something else."

"I'll bet Enzo and Maritza could tell us more about the Tavishes."

"You know," I say, inspiration looking a lot like a criminal act in this moment, "I bet they'd be home by now."

Mya looks scandalized, but not so much that she's saying *no*.

"You don't think their dad would let them hang out . . . do you?"

I shrug. "I mean, if they didn't ask, then there'd be no way for them to know for sure . . ."

Neither of us says anything after that, but somehow, we magically find our way to the front of the Esposito house, and sure enough, their dad's car is parked in the driveway.

"I mean, if this pebble just *happened* to fly up to the window of Enzo's room . . ."

"True, true," says Mya, staring at the rock in my hand. "And if they just *happen* to open the window to see what it is, it would be rude not to say anything."

"An excellent point," I say, and off the pebble flies, from my fingertips to the ledge of Enzo's window.

Unfortunately, there's another window I didn't consider: the one to the kitchen, which coincidentally is where Mr. Esposito is washing dishes and staring at my sister and me as we corrupt his kids.

The front door swings open, and there stands a stern Mr. Esposito, a pink checkered dishtowel slung over his shoulder, an angry vein throbbing in his temple.

"Aaron. Mya. Is there something I can help you with?"

Nope, not unless you have a shovel to dig us out of this latest mess I've managed to get us into.

"We were just . . . we're here because—" Mya tries, but this time, I'm faster.

"We're here to apologize," I say.

"But it was Enzo who—!" Mya starts to protest, but now isn't the time for assigning blame. It's the best excuse we've got. Besides, it was my idea to go into the forest the last time I was with Enzo, so I suppose I'm finally getting my due.

"And what is it exactly that you'd like to say sorry for?" Mr. Esposito says, his arms tight across his chest.

He's one of *those* grown-ups. He doesn't just want an "I'm sorry." He wants an "I'm sorry because." He wants reflection. Remorse.

I've just stopped my eyes from rolling all the way up in my head when I catch sight of Enzo frantically waving from the window above.

I clear my throat loudly. "Uh, Mya wanted to start by saying something," I say, nudging Mya forward like she's about to give a book report.

"Huh?"

She looks at me like I've sold her to the enemy, but I need Mr. Esposito's eyes off of me while I try to decode whatever Enzo's trying to tell me.

"Yes, sir, I, uh . . . I wanted to say that, um, it's a funny story actually, because, haha, we were, um . . ."

Mr. Esposito is starting to look a little worried about Mya, but as long as he's looking at her, he's not watching as I pretend to scratch my chin.

Enzo has a crumpled ball of paper in his hand, and I'm pretty sure he wants to drop it right in front of me, which is absolutely the worst possible idea, so I twitch my head to the side of his house and stop when Mr. Esposito shifts his focus back to me.

"Well, that's a . . . fascinating story, Mya, but that still doesn't explain why you kids thought it would be a good idea to cut through a forest with no maintained path and no parental presence so you could—what, get sick on chocolate?"

"Full-sized chocolate," I correct, and the vein in Mr. Esposito's head starts throbbing again.

I can tell Mya has now caught sight of Enzo because she's suddenly pretending to stretch but really, she's pointing to the side of the house like I did, and seriously, how is Enzo not getting this?

"But, er, you're absolutely right, sir, and we'll never do it again," I say, outright pointing to the side of the house now. "We'll never go into the forest alone. Never."

"Well, that's reassuring, Aaron, but the forest is that way," Mr. Esposito says, pointing in the opposite direction, but it worked because from the corner of my eye, I see a white paper ball sail in a high arc overhead and fall to the side of the portico, just outside of the field of Mr. Esposito's vision.

"What are you two doing out, anyway?" he asks. Apparently, it's only just occurred to him that we're the only culprits roaming free.

"Dad's on deadline," I say, and surprisingly, that's all it takes.

"Ah," Mr. Esposito says knowingly, and somehow, that doesn't make me feel better. Apparently, Dad is under as much pressure as I think he is. And that's never a good thing.

"Okay, so, bye then," I say, and it's abrupt enough that Mr. Esposito is suspicious again.

"Where are you two off to now?" he asks.

That depends entirely on what Enzo's note says.

"Eh, you know. Around," I say, and Mya nods like that's an actual answer.

But Mr. Esposito seems to have tired of us, and as luck would have it, a timer goes off in his kitchen just when I think he's going to ask us another question.

"You kids be safe. And be good," he says, emphasizing the *good* part which stings a little.

"Sorry again," says Mya, and at last, Mr. Esposito seems to soften a little.

"Stop acting your age," he scolds, a little more playfully this time, and we turn to leave on a better note, the best we can hope for anyway.

Once we hear the front door close behind us, we drop to our hands and knees, then to our bellies, and one at a time, we army-crawl across the lawn and underneath the sill of the kitchen window until we reach the side yard of Enzo's house and the crumpled note he risked life and limb to give us.

After a two-block sprint away from the Esposito house, I flatten the note on the sidewalk.

MY BACKYARD.
TONIGHT AT
7:00.
IMPORTANT

More secrets.

Mya looks at me. "So, what'll we do until then?"

Eating turns out to be the answer to that question. We venture to the Square in the middle of town and make our way around each side of it. We eat tacos and nigiri, chocolate-covered bananas and pizza bagels. We even wander over to the natural grocer when we got desperate for new scenery and give one of the weird healthy candy bars a try. By the time six forty-five arrives, I'm belching a symphony.

"Aaron, *stop*! I'm already close to puking!"

"Why do you think I'm burping so much? It's gotta come out somehow. Trust me, this is the least disgusting way."

As we near Enzo's house, I detour us around his street to approach it from the opposite side. This time, we won't have to avoid the kitchen window; we can creep over the fence and straight into the backyard.

I take a quick peek to make sure his dad isn't back there and scramble over the edge, catching myself just before I land so I can pull Mya from the top.

"Over there!"

I point to a thick hedge framing a little vegetable garden and listen for any sign of Enzo, but as each minute ticks by, we're further away from seven o'clock, and I'm more and more convinced that the plan is blown, and Mr. Esposito is going to find us.

And end us.

"Maybe this wasn't a good idea," Mya whispers, reading my mind.

"One more minute," I say, not sure I want to even wait that long. Danger has never really bothered me much. It's *stupid* danger I have a thing against.

"One more minute until what?" says a voice above us, and I lose any hint of bravery when I shriek and scramble backward.

"Shhh! Are you nuts? My dad'll hear you!" Enzo hisses, crouching behind the hedge with us.

"What took you so long?" I scold him.

"Sorry. I should have told my dad to hurry up with dinner

because I need to be on time for our secret meeting," says Enzo, frowning.

Maritza rolls her eyes and pulls Mya over to the next bush. "They're so dramatic."

"You should have heard Aaron all the way over here from the Square. 'Oh, my stomach. I have to burp, Mya. I'll explode otherwise.'"

"Oooh, you were at the Square? Did you see the bracelet I was talking about?"

Mya nods. "I bet you we could make something cooler, though. Like, something that has the same charm for you, me, and Lucy."

"Yeah, but what would the charm be?"

I look at Enzo, and he looks back at me.

"That's thirty seconds of my life I'll never get back," he says, looking back over his shoulder at his sister. "Anyway, we don't have much time. Dad had to get on some conference call, but I have no idea when that's going to end," says Enzo, pulling a photocopied page out of his pocket. It looks familiar.

"I found the old proof of this story when I was stuck cleaning out the records room."

"We actually already saw this," Mya says. "We found an old copy of it . . . um . . . at our house."

"So then, you saw the photo?"

I lean in closer. "What about the photo?"

"Look at it," he says, jamming his finger down on the page.

Just below the fold is a grainy photo of the two people I recognize as my grandparents, with Adelle's fashionable but frizzy beehive and Roger's thick-rimmed glasses and same football-player shoulders as my dad. They're both bent over a desk I immediately identify as the same one in the abandoned office from the weather station. There's something sad and vaguely creepy about seeing the entire office intact behind them. Even the hallway in the corner of the frame looks alive despite the black-and-white blur that depicts it.

Then I spot the two boys in the hallway. Or rather, I spot their heads and shoulders. The rest of them appears to have disappeared . . . into the wall.

I squint closer to be sure, but really, I don't need to. It's my dad and Mr. Gershowitz as kids, seemingly disembodied in the hallway of the weather station.

"Am I completely dense, or are their bodies gone?"

"You *are* dense, but not about this," says Enzo.

"Maybe the film got messed up," I say. "Something happened in the developing or the printing."

"Nothing else about the photo is off," says Enzo. Clearly, he's already thought this through.

"So then, what? My grandparents were actually warlocks who could make people disappear?"

Enzo blinks slowly at me, like I'm the dumbest human being on earth.

"Or, a more plausible explanation: They were walking downstairs."

I flash back to the weather station and my time there. Enzo doesn't know about any of that, and I don't see any reason why

he needs to know, but I've seen it myself. There are no stairs there.

Then I remember what he and Trinity told me on Halloween when we were in the woods.

"Wait, Trinity said the police checked that place top to bottom. There isn't a level below the ground at the weather station," I say.

"Exactly!"

Mya and Maritza crinkle their noses at us. "Shhh, dummy!" whispers Maritza.

I shake my head at Enzo. "So, if there is a secret basement, there might be something the police missed . . ."

Enzo nods. "Look, I don't think your grandparents set that fire. But they had secrets, and with you guys back in town, those secrets are going to come out."

There it is, the knot in my stomach laid bare for both of us to see. It should be super painful to see my guts splayed out like that, and mostly it is. Still, there's a part of me that's almost relieved. Not just that Enzo understands, but that he doesn't believe my grandparents were dangerous.

At least not intentionally dangerous.

"What do you know about the Tavishes?" I ask Enzo.

"I know they were rich."

"But do you know how they made their money? Like what business—"

"Caw! Caw!" Maritza calls from across the yard, and when I turn, I see her flapping her arms like wings and I think she makes a terrible bird. But her eyes are huge, and when she points one of her wings toward the back window, it becomes a little clearer, at least to me.

"What are you doing?" asks Enzo.

Maritza can't handle the stupidity. "Dad's hanging up."

Enzo pushes the photocopied article into my hands and instinctively ducks down, even though he's not crouched behind anything. Then he points to his own eyes with two fingers, then points to me, which means something like *I've got your back* I think, and Maritza joins him in his stooped form, and they soundlessly slide open the patio door and disappear inside their house, leaving Mya and me to escape on our own.

I wave her over sharply, and she scurries to the fence and makes it over the top without any help. I follow a little less gracefully. Even though it's not necessary because no one is following us, we sprint all the way home, only slowing when we reach our block.

When we open the door, it's like we were never gone. No one greets us at the door, no one looks worried or relieved or peeved or confused. No one is there at all. It's just a quiet, dark house with no proof of life.

Because we basically ate our body weight in snacks at the Square and I'm about to explode with the gas building in my intestines thanks to those nature bars, we skip the kitchen altogether and retire to our separate rooms with little more to say. What is there to discuss, really? Just one more secret to protect.

Only this time, I think I might know where to find the answers. This time, I have something to show Mr. Gershowitz, something he can't shrug off or dismiss. I know my dad is a vault, and I have zero hope I can get information from him.

But if Mr. Gershowitz can be straight with me, maybe I can steer this rumor away from my family and avoid a Titanic-level disaster.

Now all I have to do is *find* Mr. Gershowitz.

CHAPTER 12

I spent most of the night trying to figure out how to locate a ghost.

According to Dad, Mr. Gershowitz hasn't talked to him since their argument, and despite my couple of nights spent in the woods after that—in places I thought it was his job to patrol—I haven't seen any sign of him, either.

So, a ghost.

I'm so desperate to find him, I even considered asking Dad. It doesn't seem like he's all that mad at Mya and me anymore, not that either of us have seen very much of him.

But there's no way I can ask him today. Today is Unveiling Day, the day Dad's brilliant designs for the Golden Apple Amusement Park are revealed to the entire town, and then . . . well, it's probably best not to think about what comes next. One crisis at a time.

In any case, I'm on my own when it comes to finding Mr. Gershowitz.

Mya pops her head into my room without knocking.

"I could have been naked!" I say, covering myself unnecessarily.

Mya shivers. "Just the thought makes me want to tear my eyes out."

"So knock."

"Can I have your waffles?"

I take a second to switch gears. "There's waffles?"

"Mom's been calling you for like ten minutes."

The lure of maple goodness is strong, but I still haven't come up with a plan, and I don't want to face Mom and Dad before I have one.

"Hurry up. We have to leave for the unveiling at nine thirty," she says, clearly still vying for my waffle. She's ready to go, and I haven't even gotten out of pajamas yet.

"Wait, I thought Trinity said it was going to be at eleven."

"No, that's when it *starts*. We have to get there early," she says, looking over her shoulder. "Your waffles?"

"Fine, whatever," I say, and before I have a chance to realize what I've given up, she's bounding down the stairs to the kitchen.

The ceremony doesn't start until eleven. That means my family will notice if I leave midway through . . . but they won't if I'm not with them from the start.

* * *

"What kind of project?" Mom demands to know, her arms crossed tightly.

"For school," I say, just as I rehearsed in my room moments before.

Dad looks at me gloomily, like he's only just started to like me again.

"But you're going to miss the beginning!" Mom frets.

"I'll try really hard not to," I promise. "It's just that Trinity and I could only meet at this time to hand off our civics notes, and the project is almost due, and I don't want to get her in trouble, and—"

I see Mya's ears perk up when I peer over Mom's shoulder into the kitchen. She lifts her head from my plate of waffles long enough to give me a disapproving look for dragging Trinity into this. I make a mental note to apologize later—to both Trinity and Mya.

Right now, though, Trinity is my only chance to break away from the crowd without anyone noticing.

Mom sighs. "Can't you meet with her later today, after the ceremony?"

I shake my head. "She has, um, plans."

"She does?" Mya calls from the kitchen, scowling at me behind Mom's back.

"She sure does," I say, burning a hole into her as discretely as possible. "How are those waffles treating you, by the way?"

Mya puts her head back down and keeps eating, reluctantly complicit.

Up to this point, I haven't heard from Dad. I might be able to fool Mom for a short amount of time, but Dad's an entirely different story. My only hope is that he's too nervous about the ceremony to pay much attention to all the massive holes in my story, like why I never mentioned this project earlier, or how we could possibly finish it in such a short amount of time and still make it to the ceremony before it starts.

And I *have* to go now. It's the only time in the foreseeable future I'll be near the weather station. If I miss this opportunity, it'll mean courting another grounding from my parents, who forbade us to go anywhere near the woods after our last adventure. My only other option is to sneak out of the house again at nighttime, and that's just not happening again. Not if I can help it.

I take as deep a breath as I dare to, hoping Dad won't notice, and slowly tip my head to meet his eyes. I stare directly into them, with their green twinkle looking more like a spark in this moment. I try to remember when the last time is that I heard him laugh, or when I saw him smile. I try to remember when he last seemed like my dad.

Somewhere behind the green of his irises, I think I see it, that warmth, the way the skin used to crinkle around his eyes even when he wasn't smiling, the way his huge shoulders used to look protective instead of looming.

Somehow, I think I still see the old him. Somehow, somewhere.

"School comes first," he says quietly. I try so hard to read the tenor of his voice, but it tells me nothing.

We all stay silent for a moment, waiting to see if there's more, waiting to see if maybe he'll explain how he really feels.

Instead, he reaches out and presses his hand gently into my shoulder, holding my gaze, and returns to his study for his plans.

When Mom, Dad, and Mya leave, only Mya gives me a second look. She knows I'm up to something, and she probably resents being left out of it, but I need to confirm this myself first, and the memory of losing her at the weather station last time is still fresh.

"Come as soon as you can," Mom says over her shoulder, but she's more focused on my dad, who is a ball of nerves as he juggles his rolled-up blueprints and colorful presentation boards.

It takes all of my willpower, but I wait until I hear the sound of the car's engine fade to nothing before I bolt upstairs to change my clothes. Mya mercifully left me a single waffle, and I scarf it down before slamming the door behind me and sprinting down the street toward the opening to the forest.

There's no chance of getting turned around in the woods on the overgrown trails today. The noise from the gathering crowds for the Unveiling Ceremony can be heard from way back. All I have to do is follow the distant laughs and squeaking microphones they're testing for feedback.

I think it's safe to say I underestimated the importance of this celebration. It's like Raven Brooks has nothing better to do than to get excited about a bunch of blueprints.

Or maybe I just didn't want to admit that this could be Fernweh Welt times two.

As though to punish me, a blackberry vine rakes its thorny stem across my shin, tracing a deep scrape into the skin.

I bend to squeeze the cut and try to stop the bleeding, scowling at the plant all the while.

"I get it. I'm a horrible son."

I don't bother explaining to the plant that I'm just trying to keep the watchful eyes of Raven Brooks off of my obviously cursed family.

I have to stop before I even reach the future grounds of the Golden Apple Amusement Park. The crowd is so big, it's already swelled beyond the roped-off area designated for spectators, and people have trickled into the woods. Parents have set their rambunctious kids loose to chase one another between the trees, and I'm quickly realizing I'm going to need to give the area a much wider berth if I'm going to avoid being seen.

I duck from tree to tree, catching snippets of conversations as I pass.

"Now you're the dookie head!"

"Ahahahaha! I'm the dookie head! I'm the dookie head!"

"Kimberly! Marcus! Stop it! No one is a dookie head."

I pass the first obstacle, but now I'm really in the thick of it, and a cluster of teenagers has gathered around a stump at least thirty feet into the forest behind the rows of seats that face a large stage.

"I'm telling you, no one's seen him for over a week."

"There's no such thing as Forest Protectors, Jun."

"You didn't think buffalo were real until last year."

"For the last time, I thought you were talking about woolly mammoths."

"Also real."

"*Extinct!* There's a difference."

"All I'm saying is, you'd have to be crazy to go into these woods alone."

I hurry past the arguing teenagers, suddenly missing the dookie head conversation.

I'm nearly to the edge of the grounds when I stop cold because I hear my dad's voice.

And he doesn't sound happy.

"What do you expect me to do? I don't have a magic wand, Marvin."

"It's just very disappointing, Ted. I was told you were something of a miracle worker, with your ability to meet the Fernweh Welt opening deadline."

"Which was ill advised *and* five months' more time than you're giving me," Dad says. He sounds like he's practically sitting on his voice to keep it from rising.

"And you were able to hone your craft and improve your efficiency in the process," says Marvin, a man with a pair of round glasses and a round stomach to match. He's wearing a vest under his sports coat, and it looks like his buttons are really struggling. He's smiling, but not really. He's smiling like my dad is smiling.

"I'm sure this has absolutely nothing to do with your bid for mayor," says Dad, and this makes Marvin's smile slip a little.

"Careful, Ted. Careful. Wouldn't want to dig up any of the bad blood between your family and mine."

Dad's smile fades, too, and now they're just glaring at each other, waiting for the other one to say something. It looks so weird with Dad's colorful designs pinned to presentation boards behind them, all fun and family and wholesome goodness, while the two of them stare each other down, waiting for the other one to keel over.

It's Marvin who talks again.

"If you've lost your knack, Ted, we can always find someone else who needs the job."

Dad's smile creeps back in underneath his mustache, but there's nothing happy about it.

"Of course not, Marvin."

Marvin squeezes Dad's shoulder, then immediately appears to regret it because he draws it back like he's afraid Dad is going to bite him. To be honest, he probably should be a little scared.

"Can't wait to see what surprises you have in store for us," Marvin says, then hails a passing woman to drag her into some other conversation, leaving Dad all alone.

It feels like walking in on someone else's dream. I don't feel like I should have seen any of that. Dad is standing there, staring into the trees ahead of me, looking like he's anywhere else but here. I would like it so much better if he looked mad. Instead, he looks like he did when he said goodbye to me this morning.

I don't mean to take a step. Maybe it was my subconscious trying to flee. But my foot betrays me, and of course, it finds the loudest twig in all of Raven Brooks, snapping in half while the crack echoes through the patch of trees right next to the one person who absolutely *can't* see me right now.

Dad's eyes twitch, but his head doesn't move. He's like a predator, instinctively still while he relies on his senses to search out his prey.

I slowly lower myself to the ground, not that this is hiding me exactly. Maybe the leaves are a little denser by the brush, but if Dad so much as turns his head, I'm toast. There's no way he won't see me.

I have every reason to believe he'll catch me. The odds have never been stacked less in my favor than they are right now. I brace myself for his wrath, my imagination failing to conjure a punishment worse than death. Dad will think of something, though. His imagination knows no bounds.

Then, in a twist nobody could have seen coming, Dad turns around and walks in the opposite direction, his back firmly to me and the path of the forest I still have to travel.

I am one hundred percent, miraculously and inexplicably, in the clear.

I don't question it; I just run. My feet pound faster and harder than they did when I thought I was being pursued by Forest Protectors, faster than when I thought I'd lost Mya, faster than when I tried to outrun the memory of Germany and all we left undone.

I run until I literally hit a wall.

"We meet again," I say to the weather station, trying to ignore the eerie quiet that's suddenly upon me now.

Once I'm on the side of the wall with the front door, though, I see something I didn't expect.

The door is boarded up.

"What?"

* * *

Someone doesn't want me snooping anymore . . . but whether that person is Mr. Gershowitz or the developers of the theme park, or someone else entirely is anyone's guess.

"Mr. Gershowitz," I whisper, as though maybe I could conjure him by name.

It makes sense, though. He warned me about hanging around the woods, about trespassing at the weather station. And sure, that's his job, and yeah, it's probably not a good idea to stumble around an abandoned building in the dark, but there's more to it than that.

Ted, I'm telling you, things are happening. Strange things, like before . . .

Mr. Gershowitz knows there's something here to find, something my dad won't even talk about with him.

I grab the edge of one of the boards and try rattling it loose, but it won't budge. I brace my foot against the door and pull, but I can't even pry it an inch. I'm running short on hope when I remember the night I came with Mya.

Swatting at the overgrowth, I follow the wall around to the other side of the weather station, beating back the panic that I felt the last time I ran this same path. When I arrive at the place where Mya and I crashed into each other, I begin searching the wall.

Okay, maybe "searching" is the wrong word. I start slapping the wall. I'm pushing and pounding on every board to see if one shakes loose. It's impossible that Mya just spilled out of the weather station from an imaginary hole. There has to be something else here.

"There has to be something I'm not se—"

It would be so cool to say that I dove through the hole in the wall hidden behind a thick bundle of weeds and vines. Maybe I somersaulted through it, sprang to my feet like a ninja, ready for my stealth mission. It would be so cool, except there was no diving, and if there was a somersault, it was purely accidental and absolutely not ninja-like.

Nope. I fell through the hole.

But, I found the hole.

I can already tell, even in the dark, that I've never been to this part of the weather station before. It just smells different, like mold and something else I can't identify but that's equally unpleasant.

"It's not a dead body. It's not a dead body."

Still, invading thoughts of dead bodies lining the cracks of the damp hallway will probably haunt my dreams for the rest of my life.

I try to remember that Mya managed to make her way through this same hallway—in the middle of the night, no less—without completely falling apart. That helps me to keep walking without hyperventilating in the almost pitch-black passage.

At some point, the wall I'm using as my guide bends, and suddenly, I turn a sharp corner and find myself once again in familiar territory.

I've turned down a different hallway and landed myself right back where I would have started had the front door not been boarded up.

"Take that," I tell the door, but when my voice echoes all the way down the corridor, I have to stifle a shiver.

"Get a grip, Aaron," I tell myself. It's the middle of the day. It's just a building. The entire town of Raven Brooks is less than a mile away in a different part of the forest.

But they feel a million miles away, and if there's nothing to be afraid of, why is someone trying to keep me from finding something here?

I didn't realize until now that I'd been holding out some hope that the lantern in my grandparents' abandoned office would still be burning. That would at least have kept me from having to creep through the dark to get my bearings. Of course it isn't burning, though. Even if whoever was here last hadn't turned it off, surely the light would have burnt out by now.

I drag my fingertips along the damp wall until they find the doorway at the end of the corridor. Mostly, my grandparents' office appears as I left it, at least from what I can see in the teeny bit of light that's shining in from some crevice or another. But the light from the lantern isn't just burnt out.

The lantern is gone.

That shouldn't bother me, but it does.

"This was a really bad idea," I tell myself, but I have no intention of leaving. Not now, not after I've made it this far without chickening out.

I feel for the folded photocopy of the article, still pressed against the pocket of my pants, but without any light to examine it by, it does me no good. I'll just have to work from memory.

The picture that showed the shoulders and head of my dad and Mr. Gershowitz indicated that they were standing somewhere in the hallway just across from the door to my grandparents' office.

I take four steps out of the office and into the middle of the hallway, then let the darkness of the corridor swallow me completely.

I take a few more steps, reach for the opposite wall, and start moving my hands up and down the bumpy plaster.

"I don't even know what I'm looking for," I mutter, but that doesn't stop me from sliding my hands up and down, reaching high and low, inch by inch, examining every nook and cranny of the surface.

I don't want to find a basement. That's all I really know for sure. A basement means there might—*might*—have been something the police missed. Something that incriminates my grandparents.

"Maybe they were just kneeling," I say to myself about the picture from the newspaper. But the way my dad and his friend were positioned, they were definitely not kneeling. They were walking, moving downward.

I take a few more steps into the darkness, and there it is: a cut in the wall so thin, I'm not sure I would even be able to see it if I had a light. I follow the seam down to the floor, and it runs in a straight line. I follow it up and it makes a perfect right angle, then falls again to the floor.

I press the middle of the small rectangle my finger has just traced.

That's when the floor underneath me opens.

I don't know how far I fall. Ten feet? Twenty?

What I do know is that my head is hurting badly enough to make me feel like I might throw up, and the air around me smells even worse than it did in the hallway Mya found. Damp doesn't even begin to describe the heavy, wet atmosphere. I feel like I'm in a swamp, except the ground is hard and cold. I can hear the echo of a steady drip somewhere nearby, but I'm still seeing stars, and I'm not sure how I'm going to sit up.

Fear is an excellent motivator, though, and the smells and the sounds around me are unnerving enough to bring me back to consciousness.

Unsteady but on my feet, I blink hard a few times, then rub my eyes to try to bring them back into focus. Through the rhythmic pounding of my head, my vision slowly pulls into focus, and to my surprise, I can actually see through this darkness, if only a little. The walls are dark and slick looking, and slightly domed as though in the shape of a tube rather than the rectangle of a normal hallway.

This is no hallway, though.

The center of the narrow ground appears to come together at an angle, and in the middle is what at first looks like an oil slick. I bend to touch it and discover it's just water, but if I could see it better, I'm sure it would be brackish. I can feel its graininess. It doesn't run like a river. It merely sits.

The walls around me are close.

Too close.

I try to look up, to see where I fell from, but the ceiling and whatever looms above ten feet is the only thing I can't see at all. It's one giant shadow.

I have two choices: to turn around and walk into the dark, or to move forward toward a small, glowing light in the distance.

I choose the light, moving as swiftly as I dare with my head still swimming and my ears still ringing.

I'm practically on top of the wall before I see it, and when I do, I realize I'm at a T in the road, an option to turn right or left.

It's almost immediately to my left that I see the lantern.

The dome where the light emanates from is cracked and dimming, but there's no doubt in my mind that this is the camping lantern that I last saw in my grandparents' office up above. Though it wasn't cracked before.

There wasn't a dark red smear along the glass, which has dried to a crusted brown.

Without a doubt, there was not, lying right beside it, an open wallet.

I stoop to pick up the billfold, working hard to steady my hand. There, behind the little plastic window of the wallet is a driver's license, the smiling, affable face of Ike Gershowitz staring up at me.

On the little plastic window is a fingerprint, stamped in dried blood.

I look down at the deep scrape on my shin, wanting nothing more than to see it dripping blood, but whatever was there before has crusted over now. There's zero chance that the blood on Mr. Gershowitz's wallet is mine.

I don't want to remember the conversations I've overheard. I'd do anything not to remember.

I'm telling you, things are happening. Strange things, like before . . .

They were so deep into the woods, even the police couldn't believe they'd gotten that far . . .

They were so freaked, they couldn't even talk . . .

All I'm saying is, you'd have to be crazy to go into these woods alone . . .

I look down at the wallet again. A thin, high whine drifts on the dank air from somewhere I can't see—somewhere at the other end of the tunnel.

Then, without warning, the last of the light seeps from the broken lantern.

Leaving me alone in the dark, a bloody wallet from a missing man in my hand, and a howl at my back.

My stomach tightens, and a cry fills the air. When my throat starts to burn, I realize it's me who is screaming.